A KISS IN THE SNOW

"Children don't like me," Madelyn asserted. "And I don't like them."

"Is that why you let Mary keep the green hat?" Robert asked, trying not to smile.

"That was nothing," she said.

"Mary likes you."

"Only because I gave her the hat."

"That's not true. You remind her of her mother."

"Mary likes to look at my gowns. That is not the same as liking someone. Anyway, the other children don't like me. Except maybe for the little boy."

"Matthew?" He likes everyone."

"There. You see?"

"I see that you are properly blue-deviled, my dear." Robert quickly took her hand and pulled her to her feet, propelling them both into a pile of drifting snow. Before she could give voice to her indignation, he bent his head and kissed her.

She is going to slap you until your ears ring, he told himself, but he didn't care.

And to his gratification, she kissed him back, quite thoroughly. . . .

Books by Kate Huntington

THE CAPTAIN'S COURTSHIP

THE LIEUTENANT'S LADY

LADY DIANA'S DARLINGS

MISTLETOE MAYHEM

Published by Zebra Books

MISTLETOE MAYHEM

Kate Huntington

ZEBRA BOOKS
Kensington Publishing Corp.
http://www.zebrabooks.com

ZEBRA BOOKS are published by

Kensington Publishing Corp.
850 Third Avenue
New York, NY 10022

First Printing: October, 2000
10 9 8 7 6 5 4 3 2 1

Printed in the United States of America

*This book is dedicated with much love
to my husband, Robert Chwedyk,
to my parents, Max and Mary Saluke Hoch,
and to my remarkable grandmother, Mrs. Mildred Hoch.*

Prologue

Lord Blakely's Country Home, Leicestershire
December 1818

"The poor devil won't have the chance of a snowball in hell of escaping parson's mousetrap with a parcel of determined females setting mistletoe for him all over the house," protested Alexander Logan, Lord Blakely, over the remains of an excellent breakfast as his wife busied herself with a pretty profusion of red velvet ribbons, waxy white berries with small green leaves, red apples, candles, and slender wire at the other end of the dining-room table.

Kissing boughs laden with mistletoe were the end of many a bachelor's comfortable existence, but Alexander's smile was reminiscent rather than cynical. He adored his Vanessa, and she adored him. He hadn't known what happiness was until he married her.

That didn't mean, however, that his wife's childhood friend and neighbor, Robert Langtry, aspired to a similar state of connubial felicity.

Alexander was willing to bet his famous pair of matched bays that Robert's mother, Vanessa's mother, and their collective female offspring had spent many a happy hour in Yorkshire plotting the demise of Robert's freedom at the hands of the sensible widow they persuaded Vanessa to invite to the house party as well.

"How do you know they are all for Robert's benefit?" Vanessa asked coyly as she held a mistletoe sprig over her head.

Alexander strode to his wife and took her into his arms.

"Since two rather delightful results of our mutual affection are wreaking havoc in the nurseries at this moment, my darling, I would venture to say that kissing boughs are a trifle superfluous for us."

Vanessa laughed and kissed him with enthusiasm. When he looped his arm around her shoulders and would have led her to her boudoir for one of their satisfying midmorning demonstrations of that mutual affection, she gave him a sharp rap on the shoulder.

"Not now, my love," she said, sounding regretful. "I have much to do before our guests arrive."

"I agree," he said, sweeping her up in his arms, mistletoe and all, "and the most critical of these is to pay some attention to your poor, neglected husband before the hordes descend. I shan't have a moment alone with you until the New Year begins."

He was in a fair way of persuading her when their butler entered the room with the post. Alexander would have ignored him and proceeded to the stairway if Vanessa had not blushed crimson and struggled to be set down. The butler blushed, too, even after four years of serving such an unfashionably devoted couple.

"We can read the bloody post later," Alexander growled in frustration as he released his wife.

But Vanessa had already taken the post from the butler and was shuffling through the letters.

"I beg your pardon, darling?" she asked absently. Alexander sighed.

"There!" Vanessa said triumphantly, showing Alexander his father's frank on a letter. "I knew they would return to England in time for the party. The south of Italy may have its attractions, but your father is unlikely to miss Christmas with his grandsons."

Vanessa opened the letter and started reading the contents. Then she gave a muffled scream and dropped both the letter and the mistletoe on the floor.

"What is it?" Alexander asked anxiously, envisioning a fatal carriage accident or a sudden illness. "What has happened?"

"Your aunt has ruined *everything!*" she cried. "They are bringing Madelyn with them."

Alexander's brow cleared.

"Is that all? With all the people you have invited, what is one more?"

Vanessa gave her cherished husband a look of pure exasperation.

"Have you forgotten?" she asked, hands on her hips. "Robert was quite desperately in love with her, and their parting was hardly amicable. Madelyn threw a Sèvres vase at his head and followed him outside to scream her complaints after him for the edification of the neighbors as he fled from the house! Do you not remember the uproar it caused?"

"That was *years* ago, love," he said comfortingly. "He has probably forgotten all about the chit by now. And as she has spent the past two years driving every eligible bachelor on the Continent to distraction, I should be surprised if she remembers his name."

"Do you really believe that?" Vanessa asked hopefully.

"No," Alexander said with a despairing sigh. He

never could lie to Vanessa, not even to make her feel better. "Madelyn has always had the fiery temper to go with all that red hair."

"It probably was a mistake not to tell Lady Letitia that I invited the Langtrys," Vanessa said, looking troubled, "but I thought perhaps she and the earl might not come, and the children would be *so* disappointed."

Alexander had to agree with his wife's logic, if not her scruples. His father, the Earl of Stoneham, and the earl's sister, Lady Letitia, were devilish high in the instep. The party would be trying enough to their sensibilities with Vanessa's mother and lively younger sisters as fellow guests. The prospect of rubbing shoulders as well with the Whittakers' Yorkshire neighbor Robert Langtry, an undistinguished country squire, the gentleman's countrified mother, and his four extremely energetic wards could not be expected to delight them.

Alexander kissed his apprehensive wife on the forehead, coaxing a reluctant smile from her.

"I begin to see that you are right, my love, and there is not a moment to be lost," he said as he escorted her back to the partly assembled decorations on the table. "It will take a great lot of kissing boughs to interject a spirit of sweetness into *this* party!"

One

Just as the coach struggled up the snow-covered hill and came to a weary stop before the impressive entrance to Alexander and Vanessa's country home to disgorge its passengers, Robert Langtry—the lost love who had *ruined* Lady Madelyn Rathbone for all other men—ran around to the front of the house, chased by four laughing children armed with snowballs, and skidded to a halt before her.

The provoking man might have been so obliging as to grow stout, develop a peevish expression, or turn gray at the temples, but Robert Langtry was as broad-shouldered and narrow-waisted as he had been that fateful day two years ago when he refused to elope with her to Gretna Green. His blue eyes sparkled with health and good humor; his strong, square-shaped jaw and attractively cold-reddened cheekbones were all chiseled perfection. Robert's windblown hair, though innocent of Macassar oil or any of the pomades that might have kept it in decent order, was the same luxurious dark brown she remembered.

He wore an indifferently tailored coat of brown wool and a pair of scratched riding boots, but it would take more than careless grooming to make Robert Langtry look ordinary.

Before her otherwise perfectly functional brain could think of anything intelligent for her to say, Robert grabbed Madelyn, spun around to face the advancing army of children, and held her in front of him with one arm thrown across her collarbones and the other at her waist. Madelyn's hat, which she had purchased at exorbitant expense in Paris to match her elegant green velvet traveling costume, fell off her head and was carried by the wind to roll into a snowdrift.

"Abject apologies, my dear," he whispered into her ear. "I find myself in rather desperate need of a shield at the moment."

While her senses reeled from the spicy fragrance of the bay rum Robert always wore and the sudden shock of being in his arms, Madelyn found herself facing a battery of grinning children armed with snowballs ready to let fly. The coach door closed with a crisp snap as the footman shut Madelyn's godmother, Lady Letitia, inside to protect her from the firing squad. A muffled thud and indignant shriek from inside the coach told them the lady had been caught off balance, and the footman cringed.

Madelyn, although she was quite fond of her godmother and ordinarily would have been anxious to determine that the elder lady had sustained no injury, noted this with only one part of her brain.

If only Robert hadn't *touched* her.

Madelyn's heart was pounding so hard she was afraid he might hear it. She could only hope he would attribute the trembling of her limbs and the sudden moisture in her eyes to the cold, brisk wind.

To her chagrin, his hands on her were perfectly steady. There had been no emotion other than amusement in his voice.

"No prisoners!" shrieked a sturdy dark-haired girl

as she unleashed the first snowball with a battle cry worthy of a Valkyrie. Madelyn screamed and turned in Robert's arms to protect her face.

Before the snowball could hit her, Robert spun them both around with dizzying speed and gallantly shielded her with his body as the wet white stuff slammed into his back and shoulders. His cheek rested at the top of Madelyn's head, and his breath was warm on her hair. Against her face she could feel the rumble of stifled laughter deep in his chest. She closed her eyes as her body remembered what it was like to be held so tightly in his arms. She felt as if she had come home after a long journey.

"Lady Madelyn," Robert whispered after a moment. She looked up at his face, and his blue eyes twinkled with mischief as they gazed straight into hers. "I believe they've stopped."

"Oh . . . Yes . . . Of course," she said, gathering the shreds of her dignity about her. She forced her unwilling fingers to release their grip on the collar of his coat as he straightened and stepped back.

To Madelyn's dismay, the children then advanced in a giggling, jostling mass, and the oldest, a boy, dropped a handful of snow down the collar of Robert's coat. They all laughed uproariously as Robert squirmed and shouted with good-natured dismay. Madelyn remembered this boy. He had been a scruffy lad of about twelve when she last saw him. Now he was almost as tall as Robert and promised to be just as handsome.

"Here, that will do," Robert said ineffectually as the dark-haired youth and girl continued to jostle him. A husky little boy with blond hair shouted and ran around them in circles like an excited puppy. "Er, you remember my wards, do you not, Lady Madelyn?"

Madelyn looked at their animated faces uncertainly, finding it difficult to reconcile them with the same dull-eyed children who had been left in Robert's care when their parents were killed in a carriage accident three years ago. They looked so full of life. Robert, it appeared, had been an excellent guardian—or his wife had. He probably was married by now; it was plain from his jolly demeanor that Robert had not been wearing the willow for *her*. So much for his declaration that he would never love again at that last emotional meeting.

Well, she would have to put *that* out of her mind!

A small blond girl ran forward, retrieved Madelyn's hat from the snowdrift, and carefully brushed it off. She was Robert's younger niece, obviously, but Madelyn could not recall her name. It was hard for her to regard Robert's wards as individuals; rather, she thought of them collectively, as one does a mob of vandals.

Madelyn held her hand out for the hat, but the little girl gave her a teasing smile and ran off with it.

"Mary, sweetheart!" Robert called out. "Give Lady Madelyn her hat, if you please!"

The little girl pretended not to hear. The elder, dark-haired sister was watching Madelyn out of shrewd, intelligent, and not altogether approving brown eyes. Madelyn didn't remember this girl's name, either, but she remembered the look. The girl's nose and mouth were too generous and her figure was too robust for her to be considered pretty like her dainty blond sister. Rather, she was built on queenly lines, like Madelyn herself. But she would be very striking when she grew into her bold features and shed her puppy fat, Madelyn thought, which would be quite as satisfactory when she grew up.

Madelyn, a devoted worshiper on the altar of fashion, had an artist's eye that was never wrong about these things.

"She'll bring the hat back in a moment. My fault, I'm afraid," Robert said apologetically. "I attacked them first, and you got caught up in the retaliatory effort."

He smiled winsomely at her when she continued to stare at him like a brainless ninny.

"Come, now, Lady Madelyn. May we not cry friends?" he added coaxingly in that beautiful, caressing voice that had always made Madelyn's bones melt. "Vanessa will be quite put out with us if we set about to smash her crockery."

Madelyn bit her lip. The wretched man *would* remind her of that disgraceful episode.

Friends.

Such a pale word for what they once had been to one another.

"Of course. All of *that* is behind us now, thank heaven," she said, forcing a polite, indifferent smile to her lips.

What else *could* she say? That her girlish infatuation for him had not abated one whit after all these years?

She would rather die!

He's probably married, Madelyn reminded herself sternly as she fought an ardent desire to burrow back into his arms. *I will* not *make a fool of myself in front of this man!*

She collected herself with an effort and turned away from Robert's smiling face when the footman, with a comical look of dread on his face, opened the carriage door to reveal a sputtering Lady Letitia on all fours. Her stylish hat listed precariously to one side.

"Stop that," she snarled as she rose clumsily to her

feet and impatiently batted away her dresser's hands when she tried to straighten her employer's headgear and pat her coiffure into some sort of order.

"Lady Letitia! You are not hurt?" Madelyn exclaimed, conscience-stricken. Her godmother's plight had completely left her mind while she was in Robert's arms.

"Hardly." Lady Letitia sniffed as she accepted the footman's hand and descended the carriage steps with all the self-assurance of a queen. She gave the poor fellow a look that would have curdled milk.

"Mr. Langtry," Lady Letitia said glacially as she pointedly ignored the hand Robert had extended to assist her from her other side. Normally she never frowned for fear such rash emotion might manifest itself in wrinkles on her remarkably well preserved countenance, but she made an exception on this occasion. It almost made her look her true age. "I did not expect to see *you* here. I suppose those . . . children are your wards."

"Indeed, my lady," he acknowledged. "I should be delighted to present them to you."

"Pray do not! How very *big* they are grown," she sniffed, as if this were the very height of vulgarity.

"I hope you are well, Lady Letitia," Robert said politely enough, although his smile had hardened.

"Quite," the lady said in unmistakable dismissal as she turned to Madelyn. "Are you all right, my dear?" she asked sympathetically. "Perhaps you should have someone show you to your room at once so you can lie down."

"Certainly not," said Madelyn, embarrassed by her godmother's rudeness to Robert and his wards. "The only damage was to my dignity and perhaps my hat."

She looked around for the object in question and saw the little blond girl preening and prancing about in the borrowed finery. Madelyn was surprised she didn't fall down, for the hat, with its graceful plumes and heavy deep pink velvet roses, kept dipping forward to cover her eyes. The child's own bonnet was hanging from her back by its strings.

The green velvet hat was safe enough for now, Madelyn decided as she returned her attention to Robert.

She couldn't seem to take her eyes off him.

Robert's smile faded, and he gave her a questioning look. Madelyn decided she would have to say something conventional and indifferent, preferably without stammering, *at once*, or he would know how much the mere sight of him discomposed her.

To her relief, the Earl of Stoneham and Mr. Cedric Wyndham provided a distraction by riding up behind the coach on their horses.

Poor Mr. Wyndham, she thought guiltily.

He would still be basking in the warm Neapolitan sunshine if Madelyn had not suddenly decided to return to England with the earl and his sister after their visit to her at her rented villa in Naples. He probably agreed to Lady Letitia's suggestion that he accompany them in the hope that Madelyn would accept the marriage proposal he extended to her several months ago, even though her reply had been evasive.

Madelyn knew Mr. Wyndham infinitely would have preferred to join the ladies inside the coach with a hot brick at his feet and an appreciative audience for his polished compliments, but the younger man could hardly cosset himself against the brisk chill of the day once the earl, who was nearly thirty years his senior, professed a desire for fresh air and announced his intention of making the last leg of the journey on horseback.

Mr. Wyndham was the first to admit he was no

outdoorsman, and Madelyn tried very hard not to despise him for it.

Madelyn gladly would have taken his place at the earl's side. She saw many beautiful lands in her two years of wandering the Continent, but nothing looked, nothing felt, nothing *smelled,* like England in winter. The ice and snow clung to the trees and turned them to marvels of crystal and spun sugar. Unfortunately, Madelyn could hardly leave her godmother to ride alone in the earl's coach with only their maids for company after Lady Letitia's many kindnesses to her. Madelyn's own traveling coach containing her gowns and the gentlemen's valets followed.

Madelyn gave Mr. Wyndham a reassuring smile as he returned a pleasant response to the earl's cheerful comment that there was nothing like being on horseback after a good snowfall to clear a man's head of the crotchets.

Cedric Wyndham would be an excellent match for her, as Lady Letitia never tired of pointing out. Madelyn had been an irresistible, if illusive, target for matchmakers ever since her brilliant debut at the age of sixteen, but it presented a decidedly *off* appearance for a lady of high estate to reach the age of nearly one-and-twenty without selecting a husband. All of the debutantes with whom she had made her bows at court were married long ago. Madelyn supposed they had been laughing behind their hands at her failure to find a suitable husband for years.

Mr. Wyndham's pedigree as the eldest son of Viscount Barlowe was unexceptionable, even if the estate he expected to inherit was not as impressive as any of the three Madelyn herself possessed. Some might say the daughter of an earl should look higher for a husband than a minor diplomat, but Mr. Wyndham's more modest prospects suited Madelyn to the ground.

If she were ill-bred enough to boast of such con-
quests, Madelyn could number several wealthy, titled
noblemen both in England and on the Continent
among her rejected suitors. It was true that Lady Letitia's hopes of the handsome and urbane Count Andreas Briccetti for Madelyn did not come to fruition,
much to that lady's disappointment. She dearly
would have loved to boast to all her acquaintance of
her holidays on the Tyrrhenian Sea at the villa of
her goddaughter, the count's bride. Marrying Count
Briccetti would have been a triumph, but Madelyn
consoled herself with the reflection that a gentleman
of such high estate would certainly expect to rule
the roost, and Madelyn did not choose to regulate
her life according to any man's whim.

Mr. Wyndham needed Madelyn far more than she
needed him, and this added considerably to his de-
sirability as a consort.

Moreover, the gentleman was quite handsome,
having blue eyes—but not, alas, as blue as Robert's—
and abundant blond curls that caused susceptible females to cast him languishing looks. His figure was
elegant. His manners were flawless. He would defer
to her in all things.

What else could she possibly want in a husband?

Love, Madelyn admitted to herself with an inward
sigh of despair.

How utterly pathetic.

"Do go into the house," she said to Lord Stoneham and Lady Letitia when she noticed they were
waiting for her to accompany them. In spite of everything, Madelyn couldn't bring herself to walk away
from Robert quite yet. Her frantic brain searched for
a logical reason to remain with him, and happily her
eyes fastened on the little girl wearing her green vel-

vet hat. "I will join you as soon as my property is restored to me," she said.

The earl nodded and moved on immediately, but Lady Letitia did not accept her brother's arm until it became evident that Mr. Wyndham intended to remain rooted to Madelyn's side with his usual dog-like devotion.

"Come along, Uncle Robert! We have not begun to take our revenge!" the dark-haired girl cried, seizing her uncle's arm and trying to drag him away. Madelyn could tell from the girl's narrowed eyes that she was anxious to remove her uncle from an immediate source of danger. The older children had made it perfectly clear right after they came to live with Robert that Madelyn was not acceptable to them as their guardian's wife, even though she had tried to woo them with smiles and expensive presents.

Neither they nor Robert were about to forgive her for suggesting that Robert send them to boarding school.

There is *nothing* wrong with boarding school, Madelyn thought defensively. *She* had been the resident of a select boarding school for most of her childhood while her father served his country, first as a general in the army and later at various diplomatic postings throughout Europe. Of course, Madelyn's mother, an ambitious lady with a lively sense of adventure, insisted upon accompanying him on these assignments. The botheration of dragging a child all over the world would have been vastly inconvenient; Madelyn understood this perfectly well now that she was an adult.

Madelyn had missed her parents very much at first, but she received a first-rate education and thoroughly enjoyed the companionship of other girls her age once she had grown accustomed to the place.

Boarding school, therefore, seemed the logical solution for a bachelor left with the dilemma of four children on his hands, or so it seemed to Madelyn. He admitted at the time he knew nothing about children, and Madelyn merely was trying to be helpful.

"*Please*, Uncle Robert!" the smaller blond-haired boy coaxed as he grabbed Robert's other arm. "You promised to take us sledding."

"In a moment," Robert said. He waved to the little girl who was still wearing Madelyn's hat. "Bring the hat here, if you please, Mary."

The little girl shook her head playfully and hid the hat behind her back, skipping back a few steps and grinning at Robert in unmistakable invitation for him to chase her.

"Please, darling," Robert coaxed. The little girl grinned and skipped back a few more steps.

"I'll get it for you, Uncle Robert," the husky boy shouted as he sprinted off in pursuit. Mary squealed and ran while the older children shouted encouragement.

"Mary! I believe your father asked you to return the hat to the lady," a strong female voice barked through the cacophony of the children's high spirits.

Madelyn flinched, for she had not seen the woman approach. Whatever her relationship was to Robert and these children, she sounded like someone who expected to be obeyed.

Mary skidded to a halt so abruptly that her brother ran into her. They tumbled to the ground, but the girl rolled like a porcupine around the hat to protect it. One of the plumes was bent at a crazy angle when she stood up. She thrust her lower lip out in defiance at the woman, and the other children regarded the interloper with surly expressions.

Madelyn remembered those surly expressions all

too well, even though *she* had done nothing to deserve them.

"Apologize at once," the woman commanded. Her lips were smiling, but her eyes were stern. The combination made Madelyn's flesh creep. "I am persuaded you do not wish to embarrass your uncle in front of Lord Blakely's guests!"

Mary gave Robert a look of apology, and at an infinitesimal signal from him, she moved to obey. Madelyn could see a sprinkling of tears on the child's eyelashes as she held out the hat to Madelyn.

"I'm sorry, ma'am," she whispered.

"No harm done. I am much obliged to you for brushing it off for me," Madelyn said to the little girl as she accepted the hat. She found that woman's officiousness most annoying. If Robert chose not to reprimand his niece, what business was it of *hers?*

Unless, Madelyn thought with dismay, that woman was his wife!

"I will buy you a new hat," Robert said quietly to Madelyn as he caressed the little girl's damp blond ringlets.

"Nonsense. It is only a bit wet, and my maid can replace the plume easily enough." Madelyn lifted her eyebrows at the unfamiliar woman, who was engaged in brushing snow off the back of Robert's coat and fussing over him as if she had a right.

"Look at you, Mr. Langtry," she scolded fondly. "You are as bad as one of the children!"

She was attractive enough, Madelyn thought wryly, if one admired primly dressed females with oppressively restrained dark hair, penetrating gray eyes, and slightly predatory expressions.

"You must forgive our Mary," the woman added, giving Madelyn a wide, insincere smile. "The little dear is *so* fond of pretty things." She said this as if the child were to be pitied for such a sad failing.

"I do not believe we have been introduced, Miss . . ." Madelyn said to the woman.

"Forgive me," said Robert, looking uncomfortable. "Lady Madelyn, may I present Mrs. Crowley, our neighbor from Yorkshire? Her late husband was the pastor of our church."

Not his wife but a widow, Madelyn thought with relief. That explained the proprietary air. Madelyn had no doubt that a well-to-do country squire would be quite a catch for a clergyman's widow.

"Mr. Wyndham," Madelyn said, turning to her escort in order to draw him into the conversation. He had retreated several steps and regarded the children with dismay, as if he thought they might bite.

Madelyn could sympathize completely.

"This is Mr. Robert Langtry, a friend of our hostess's family, and Mrs. Crowley." She watched the polite smile harden on Robert's face. "Mr. Wyndham," she added, taking that gentleman's arm and smiling up into his face, "was kind enough to escort us home from Italy. He was lately attached to one of our country's embassies in Africa."

Mr. Wyndham all but simpered in gratification, and the gentlemen exchanged wary bows.

Mrs. Crowley thrust herself forward.

"And I," she said, with a flourish of one bluntnailed, capable hand, "am pleased to present my daughters, Laura and Aimée."

Madelyn had noticed the unnaturally quiet, neatly dressed little girls who were standing shyly behind their mother. Not a soft brown curl on their little heads was out of place, and they wore matching coats of blue wool with white hats and mittens. Under their mother's critical gaze, the girls performed identical, precisely correct little curtsies.

"How perfectly charming," said Mr. Wyndham, smiling upon the little girls.

The widow's daughters reminded Madelyn of perfectly trained lapdogs. They looked with faint anxiety at their mother, as if seeking approval.

Mrs. Crowley glowed with triumph at this demonstration of her children's docility.

Madelyn felt sorry for Robert's wards, who shuffled their feet and hunched their shoulders as if they knew they had been judged and found wanting. The older girl was openly sneering.

"I am afraid I don't remember all the children's names, Mr. Langtry," Madelyn said, smiling at them. "Will you not introduce them to us?"

Robert looked pleased.

"Lady Madelyn, Mr. Wyndham, these are my wards, Mark, Melanie, Mary, and Matthew." As each name was called, the proper child gave an awkward little bow or appealingly flawed curtsy. Robert, apparently finding nothing amiss, beamed proudly.

It occurred to Madelyn that although Robert's wards were hardly perfect in either appearance or manners, they were trying very hard to do their uncle credit.

Madelyn smiled and on impulse formally curtsied to them as Mr. Wyndham favored them with a stiff nod.

When she rose, she felt a little tug on her skirts and saw that Mary was trying to claim her attention.

"Will you teach me how to curtsy like that?" she asked, her eyes shining. Mary's eyes were the very color and shape of Robert's.

"I should be delighted," Madelyn was surprised to hear herself say. She was even more surprised to realize that she meant it. "Perhaps you would like to take charge of this for me."

Madelyn gave her hat back to the gratified little blond girl. Mary immediately plopped it on her head and pranced triumphantly ahead of Madelyn and Mr. Wyndham as they walked to the front door.

Robert's jaws were aching from the strain of keeping a smile on his face by the time he could escape to the solitude of his room for a moment. It was a relief to stop trying to pretend as if his whole world hadn't taken a precarious dip on its axis.

Lady Madelyn was even more beautiful than he remembered, with her bright red hair, brilliant green eyes, and the voluptuous figure that drove him mad encased in emerald green velvet. Whereas before she merely had been a lovely girl filled with promise, now she was a woman in the full bloom of her confidence and power.

When he arrived at Lord Blakely's house and learned that Lady Madelyn was expected, Robert honestly thought he could see her again without making a bloody fool of himself, even though it had taken him *years* to get over seeing her face every night just before he went to sleep; *years* to stop despising himself for making her so unhappy.

She had been so young, so innocent, beneath her veneer of polished sophistication. She had not been discouraged in the least when her guardian refused Robert's suit for her hand.

They would simply elope to Scotland!

She would, herself, pay the person who performed the ceremony so no one would later accuse Robert of taking advantage of her and have the marriage put aside.

What an innocent she had been.

Everyone would accuse him of taking advantage of her, and the gossips would eat her alive! The beautiful, accomplished Lady Madelyn had always been society's darling. How could Robert let her be ostracized by all of the polite world merely because he needed her as he needed his next breath?

He knew she would regret marrying him. She would have to live with him and his wards on his mother's modest estate in Yorkshire the year around because marrying without her guardian's permission before she came of age would result in the forfeiture of her entire fortune. There would be no more *tôn* parties, no more Seasons in London, no more summers at fashionable resorts, no more lovely clothes made by the most expensive dressmakers in the world.

When he tried to make her understand, she swallowed her pride and *begged* him to marry her. Madelyn did not care the snap of her fingers if she lost her fortune, she protested. She wanted only him.

But Robert cared. He cared very much.

Not because of *him* would Madelyn lose all the comfort and luxury she deserved and had every right to expect. Not because of *him* would all of London laugh at her. If he permitted it, she would hate him someday.

Madelyn had been so angry. So hurt. She accused him of wanting her only for her fortune.

As if he cared a rap for her bloody fortune!

Robert gave an audible groan.

She had looked absolutely stunned when she saw him that afternoon.

And did he bow and greet Lady Madelyn properly, like a gentleman worthy of her acquaintance?

Oh, no. Not *he*.

He just reached out and *grabbed* her because he couldn't keep his greedy hands away from her for a moment longer. She had been speechless with indignation at his effrontery, as well she might!

He was a fool! An idiot! An *imbecile!*

It had seemed innocuous enough to accept an invitation to Lady Blakely's house party, even though he knew perfectly well there was a scheme afoot to marry him off to Pamela Crowley. Robert certainly had not missed the significance of the mistletoe suspended from every doorway and chandelier in the house, and he had not hesitated to go along with tradition and steal a kiss or two from the pretty widow.

In a moment of weakness he even thought it might be pleasant to court a sensible woman who would be satisfied with a husband possessed of an adequate, but by no means princely, income. Mrs. Crowley would be content to queen it in provincial society, and she would do her duty by him and his wards with her usual efficiency. She was an excellent housewife, and his mother approved of her, which made Pamela Crowley unique among all the marriageable ladies of his acquaintance.

Unfortunately, Robert could never marry Pamela Crowley—or, indeed, anyone else—now that he had seen Madelyn again. And Madelyn would be a fool to have him. Although he was not yet thirty, Robert sometimes felt like an exhausted old man. His wards, much as he loved them, were a rare handful.

Madelyn deserved better than Robert as a bridegroom, and she obviously realized it now.

Robert hadn't missed the way she took Mr. Wyndham's arm and smiled up at him through her lashes.

Mr. Wyndham, from the top of his heavily pomaded blond hair to his gleaming boots, was everything Robert was not.

If Madelyn meant to have him, Robert would just have to pretend he didn't care.

Two

Madelyn would have been taken aback herself if she hadn't caught a glimpse of Mr. Wyndham's face. Instead, she found it hard not to laugh.

He was absolutely horrified.

No doubt he had envisioned the civilized sort of country house party at which everyone behaves with perfect decorum all day and the gentlemen, after being regaled by their host with naughty stories and fortified with copious quantities of port after dinner, tiptoe to their chosen ladies' boudoirs in order to indulge in a discreet bit of romantic intrigue.

Instead, the house was teeming with children, and the shrill laughter of their overexcited little voices was quite a shock to the nerves when Lord Blakely's stately butler opened the thick, beautifully carved oak door, festooned with pine boughs and holly, to admit them.

Their hostess's younger sisters, Aggie and Amy, who Madelyn guessed must be ages eleven and twelve by now, chased a pair of sturdy, rosy-cheeked, dark-haired toddlers, whom Lady Madelyn instantly recognized from their proud grandfather's description as the celebrated Masters James and Jeremy Logan, Vanessa and Alexander's twin sons, through the impressive, marble-floored entrance hall. Madelyn had left the country before these boys were born. A large, shaggy dog of undetermined parentage was barking and trying to lick whatever jam-colored, sticky substance was liberally decorating their faces and chubby little fingers. Mary Langtry gave a shriek and ran farther into the house when one of the boys noticed the green velvet hat and approached her with his gummy hands outstretched for it.

His little mouth opened to release an indignant wail at being thwarted of the prize, but he spotted his grandfather at that moment, and the wail became an enthusiastic squeal of excitement. The Earl of Stoneham's London acquaintances would have stared to see that dignified gentleman drop to his knees and spread his arms wide for his squealing grandsons' affectionate hugs, oblivious to the ruination of his exquisitely arranged neckcloth. His habitual expression of aristocratic hauteur melted like wax.

"Lady Madelyn, I'm so pleased you could join us," said Vanessa with a bright, determined smile on her face after she had properly greeted the earl and his sister. Vanessa's sharp, sideways glance at Lady Letitia told Madelyn she knew exactly whom to blame for the addition of two uninvited houseguests to her party.

"Mr. Wyndham was kind enough to escort us from the Continent," Lady Letitia said without a blush, "and I was certain you would be delighted if we brought him along, for handsome bachelors are always in such short supply, alas, at parties."

"Too true," said Vanessa with a gracious smile for the gentleman. "Good afternoon, Mr. Wyndham. It is pleasant to see you again. We are well acquainted with Mr. Wyndham," she added to Lady Letitia and Madelyn, "because of his work in the diplomatic service."

Mr. Wyndham preened; Vanessa paused to give a surreptitious warning glance at her husband, who had just arrived on the scene to stare incredulously at Mr. Wyndham before he schooled his features to resemble a polite mask.

"Good afternoon, Mr. Wyndham. Welcome." Beneath the smile, Alexander appeared to be gritting his teeth. His glare at Lady Letitia told Madelyn they would be having words later.

Mr. Wyndham smiled winsomely at him and shook hands, but when his host moved on and Vanessa explained the room arrangements, the corners of his mouth turned down in an expression of discontent. It made him look quite sour.

Madelyn raised her eyebrows at him, and he was instantly all smiles again. Did he think she had missed the look of glacial displeasure he directed at their hostess when he realized that he and Madelyn were situated at quite opposite ends of the house? Certainly, for an unexpected guest he was quite choosy.

"I hope you will not mind staying in the nursery wing, Lady Madelyn," Vanessa was saying apologetically. "All of the rooms in the west wing are occupied except for one, and I am persuaded it would be best to put Mr. Wyndham there. Mrs. Langtry and Mrs. Crowley are also in the nursery wing, for they are quite inseparable friends."

Certainly they are, Madelyn thought cynically. She had no doubt that Mrs. Langtry was excessively popular with husband-hunting females eager to ingratiate themselves with the mother of such a desirable bachelor. Moreover, the proximity of the older woman's room to those of the only unmarried female visitors in the house guaranteed that there would be no improper visits from ardent gentlemen in the night, which suited Madelyn just fine.

It was plain that Mr. Wyndham presumed too much.

"Do not apologize, Lady Blakely. I am certain we shall be quite comfortable," Madelyn said politely as she prepared to follow the housekeeper to her quarters.

Madelyn was pleasantly surprised when the housekeeper ushered her into a spacious and meticulously clean suite, even if the furnishings were a trifle outmoded. It would do nicely. She had said something complimentary and dismissed the housekeeper when she heard her maid's voice lowered conspiratorially. Bettina was somewhat hard of hearing, so her whispers carried quite clearly.

"You will have to go now," she heard her maid tell someone in the adjoining room. "I hear my lady."

Madelyn followed her maid's voice to find Mary Langtry sitting on the embroidered ivory counterpane of a large four-poster bed draped with rose-pink silk hangings, eagerly examining Madelyn's freshly unpacked gowns as the maid carefully placed them in the clothespress. The green velvet hat was in the child's lap.

Both looked guilty when they saw Madelyn.

"I see you have found an assistant, Bettina," Madelyn said mildly.

A shy smile lit the little girl's face.

"You have such beautiful clothes, ma'am," she said wistfully as she touched the Belgian lace at the throat of Madelyn's most expensive afternoon gown with a careful finger. The child had taste, at any rate. "Just like my mother's things."

"Thank you, Miss Mary," Madelyn said graciously. She recalled that the child's late mother, Eleanor

Langtry, had been quite beautifully turned out when she appeared in society. There probably was little glamour in the girl's life now that she was living in the wilds of Yorkshire with her bachelor uncle and his old-fashioned mother.

"My lady is weary from her long journey, miss," said Bettina in a voice that brooked no argument, "and she will want to rest now."

"Yes, Bettina," the child said with obvious regret as she carefully placed the green hat on the counterpane. Mary's feet did not quite touch the ground, so Madelyn helped her down from the bed.

The little girl was surprisingly light and agile, like a cat. And the tiny hands she placed on Madelyn's arms were warm and sweetly clinging.

She disarmed Madelyn completely by saying dreamily, "You smell so wonderful," as Madelyn put her on the floor. Then she scampered to the door and looked back over her shoulder with a winsome smile.

"I may come back, mayn't I?"

"Of course," said Madelyn uncertainly. After all, what *could* she say?

When the little girl disappeared in a flutter of muslin skirts, Bettina gave Madelyn an anxious look.

"I thought it would do no harm just to let her see your gowns as I put them away, my lady," said the maid. She looked as if she expected a severe scold.

"No harm at all," Madelyn agreed. "Do help me out of this costume. I have worn it so long, it feels as if it is melded to my skin."

"Yes, my lady," said the maid.

"A word with you, Aunt Letitia, if you please," said Alexander with a determined look in his eye as he took the elder lady's arm and guided her toward an adjoining parlor.

His lips might be smiling, but his voice had steel behind it.

"Dearest, it was such a tedious journey," she said, holding a languid hand to her brow. "I am certain you will pardon me if I go straight to my bed." She sighed and fluttered her eyelashes in mock weariness; her provoking nephew merely gave a short, rude snort of laughter.

"Spare me the airs and graces, my dear aunt, for we both know you have the vitality of a woman half your age, particularly when it pleases you to cause mischief," he said, shutting the door with sufficient force to make his aunt wince. "Now. Tell me what could have possessed you to bring that mincing man-milliner Cedric Wyndham into my home."

"What possible objection can you have to Cedric Wyndham?" Lady Letitia asked in a tone of bewildered innocence. "He is a charming young man who has distinguished himself in diplomatic circles by representing His Majesty's government in several foreign countries."

Alexander rolled his eyes.

"Did *he* tell you that?" he asked, indicating with a casual wave of his hand that she was to sit down on the sofa while he sprawled in a leather chair and stretched out his long legs before him. "If that don't beat the Dutch! And I suppose you have encouraged him to sniff around Madelyn's skirts—"

"Alexander!" His aunt sniffed in disapproval. "I will thank you not to use such vulgar expressions in my presence!"

"Your pardon," he said, conceding her point with an ironic inclination of his head. "I suppose he neglected to mention that he was posted to the most unpleasant, disease-infested backwater that has the honor to enjoy diplomatic relations with the British government because he single-handedly almost destroyed relations between England and Russia on one of his first assignments."

"You must be mistaken!" Lady Letitia exclaimed. "Why did I know nothing of this?"

"Because the government was eager to hush the whole disgraceful affair. Your precious Mr. Wyndham was attached to the Grand Duchess of Oldenburg's party when she visited London for the Peace Celebrations in 1814, and the silly cawker had the infernal conceit to fancy the great lady wanted *him* as her next husband.

"Grand Duke Cedric," he scoffed. "Sounds impressive, does it not? He boasted in his cups that his joining the Russian imperial family would mean great things for England! The fellow made an ass of himself and infuriated the grand duchess to the point that Wyndham's superior had no choice but to banish the idiot to a post where he could not do much damage until the furor died down. Fortunately for Wyndham, his father is not without influence at Whitehall. Otherwise, he would have been discharged from the diplomatic service in disgrace."

"Do you honestly expect me to believe a *word* of that outlandish story?" Lady Letitia demanded with a sniff.

"Yes, because I have never lied to you," Alexander said, looking her straight in the eye.

Lady Letitia bit her lip. Alexander had infallible sources of information in government circles, and it was true he never lied, not even when the merest civility would compel him to do so. It was quite one of his most exasperating character flaws.

"I was certain he would make Madelyn a charming

husband," she said defensively. "It is past time for Madelyn to marry, and *this* suitor, at least, is not likely to cry off and leave her to face the embarrassment of a broken engagement."

Alexander stiffened.

"I suppose you blame *me* because I did not offer for Madelyn myself after you and Father told all of your acquaintance that we were betrothed from our cradles. Madelyn herself never considered me a serious suitor, and you know it!"

"The two of you would have made a charming couple if you had not become infatuated with that Vanessa Whittaker," Lady Letitia declared.

"Marrying *that Vanessa Whittaker* was the wisest thing I've ever done," Alexander said stiffly, "and I will thank you not to make spiteful remarks about my wife."

"And then that odious cousin of your wife's disappointed her, too—"

"Madelyn and Edward Whittaker would have murdered each other within the twelvemonth. They are both stubborn as bedamned."

"Language, Alexander," Lady Letitia murmured in a tone of long suffering.

"Your pardon," he said sarcastically. "A match between them would have been a disaster."

"Precisely! But Mr. Wyndham is not like that. He defers to Madelyn in all things—"

"And permits her to walk roughshod over him anytime she pleases," Alexander said in disgust. "A felicitous arrangement, to be sure."

"Well, it *will* be if you would kindly restrain yourself from interfering in something that is none of your affair!" Lady Letitia snapped.

At that she rose to her feet and stalked to the door, slamming it behind her with such force that she

quite spoiled the impression of frailty she had been
at such pains to cultivate in order to get around her
disagreeable nephew.

"She is the enemy," said Melanie, gathering her
troops around her. Mary's head was bowed in an at-
titude of abject guilt as she stood before her accusing
sister. *"All* of them are enemies. How could you have
forgotten?"

"She reminds me of Mama," said Mary, her eyes
pleading for understanding.

Melanie snorted.

"She is *not* like Mama! They don't want us, any of
them," Melanie said. "They only want to marry Uncle Robert, and Lady Madelyn is the most dangerous
of them all."

The Langtry children were well accustomed to ladies who plied them with sweets and affection as a
means of ingratiating themselves with their eligible
uncle. Normally it was no great chore to vanquish
them, for Uncle Robert saw through their stratagems
with ease. Mrs. Crowley, for example, was doing her
best to convince him that he needed a strong woman
to nag his children into good behavior and organize
his household. Luckily, Uncle Robert didn't want a
woman introducing order and discipline into his life
any more than they did, thank heaven!

But Lady Madelyn was a different problem altogether. She wasn't going to bring them biscuits or
fresh-baked cakes like those other hopeful women.
She didn't act coy and kittenish around Uncle
Robert. She didn't have to.

His eyes looked different when she was near.

His voice sounded different.

And that hadn't changed after all these years.

Despite Grandmother's contention that only a royal duke would be high enough to satisfy Lady Madelyn's overweening conceit, Melanie was sure Lady Madelyn wanted him. *All* the ladies wanted Uncle Robert.

Lady Madelyn might be all cool and aloof when she was around him; she might cling to the arm of that other yellow-haired stick of a gentleman, but she would have to be an idiot if she didn't know Uncle Robert was the best person in the world.

One could tell by the clothes she wore and the way everyone practically bowed down and let her walk on their backs that Lady Madelyn was accustomed to having anything she wanted.

Well, she wasn't going to have Uncle Robert!

Melanie had seen Lady Madelyn on only three occasions in those horrible days after their parents were killed. The first was just afterward, when she came to call on them. She actually brought them presents. Melanie had been numb. Her whole world had been shattered. Yet here was this exquisitely dressed female sitting in her mother's parlor smiling and giving them presents, just as if *that* would make up for what had happened. Then, later, she came to the funeral, and Uncle Robert went away with her to a private room when he thought no one would notice. He came back looking sad and defeated.

Melanie thought they had seen the last of her until the following Christmas, when she again came bearing gifts, but they showed her they saw through her tricks. Lady Madelyn had left in tears, and Melanie thought they had vanquished her for good.

Now she was back to insinuate herself into their lives. Melanie hadn't forgotten that Lady Madelyn tried to persuade Uncle Robert to send them to boarding school. She heard him tell Grandmother one evening when they thought the children were all asleep.

She was a shrewd one, was Lady Madelyn. She had won over Mary, but Mary was easy to bamboozle. She was pretty and innocent and would make a spectacular match when she grew up, Melanie thought bitterly. Everyone said so.

Mary is such a dear girl, Mrs. Langtry. So delicate. So sweet. So eager to please. What beautiful blue eyes she has.

Not like Melanie. Melanie had dark hair, and there was nothing delicate about her. Her eyes were brown, like mud; not blue, like the summer sky. Nobody thought *she* was pretty except those women who came with lies in their mouths to impress Uncle Robert.

"She's very beautiful," said Mark.

Melanie scowled at him. He was talking about Lady Madelyn, of course.

Her brother was fifteen, and he was slowly turning into one of *them*. Ever since his voice had deepened and Uncle Robert arranged for the curate to start training him for university, Mark had been someone else.

"That's all right for you to say," Melanie snapped. "You will be going to university, and *we* are the ones who will be sent away to boarding school. Uncle Robert will go off with Lady Madelyn and forget all about us. Then we truly will be orphans."

Her younger brother, Matthew, looked apprehensive.

"Uncle Robert promised he would never leave us," he said.

"Lady Madelyn can make him forget that," Melanie said grimly. "Men! Show them a pretty face and they lose all reason. And she is more crafty than the others. She is playing hard to get. You mark my words."

"She is *nice,*" Mary said wistfully. "She said I could go back and see more of her gowns and jewels. Melanie, she has so *many,* just like Mama."

"Is that all you can think about? Gowns and jewels?" Melanie said in disgust as a lump formed in her throat. She missed her mother's gentle hugs and kisses, her soft voice, the perfume that surrounded her like a fragrant cloud. When Mama died, all the beauty went out of Melanie's life.

Lady Madelyn might wear beautiful clothes and positively reek of expensive French scent, but she *wasn't* like Mama.

She didn't think Melanie was special at all. None of them did.

They only saw the body that had betrayed her by growing stout and awkward.

They only saw the heavy black hair that refused to curl no matter how tightly it was papered.

They only saw the spots that marred her face and made her ugly.

This happened after her mother's death, but Melanie knew her mother would have loved her, anyway. She would have given Melanie a hug and told her that spots were the reason the Almighty had given women cosmetics.

Melanie had no delusions about what her life would be like once she was under the thumb of a surrogate stepmother. None of the women really loved them or Uncle Robert. They just wanted to get married. Mrs. Crowley, especially. Laura had told Melanie that if Mrs. Crowley didn't find a husband soon, they would have to move away and live with their mean old grandmother, who would resent every crust of bread they put in their mouths. Mrs. Crowley's parents were rich, and they had not approved of Laura's papa because he was a man of the church instead of a lord.

Laura and Aimée *wanted* their mother to marry again, the little ninnyhammers.

Mrs. Crowley was forever parading her perfectly behaved little girls in front of Uncle Robert. She had even told him that the girls looked upon him quite as a father.

Such rubbish. Those girls wouldn't say boo to a goose.

To do Uncle Robert justice, he wasn't like those other men who merely tolerated their own children for the sake of getting to be the head of a family and put on airs in the neighborhood.

He really loved his wards—even Melanie, although she could tell he often didn't know quite what to make of her. He took all his meals at home with them, played with them outside so that any neighbor calling on them could see him doing so, and visited them each evening before they went to bed to hear them recite their lessons and tell the younger ones a story.

Melanie was too big for a story, and she pretended not to be paying attention, but she listened, anyway.

Grandmother was sweet, but she was the first to admit she could never rear the children on her own. She had needed someone to take care of *her* even before Mama and Papa died, and that someone had always been Uncle Robert. Grandmother thought Uncle Robert was lonely and needed a sensible wife to help raise them to be ladies and gentlemen instead of wild little ruffians, as she sometimes called them when she was tired, but she was wrong.

Uncle Robert wasn't lonely at all. He had *them*! They loved him so much. He was their whole world.

"We must not let them be alone together," Melanie said, looking each sibling in the eye. "If we can just keep them apart until we have to go home, they will forget all about each other."

Mark gave her that knowing man smile, the one Melanie so distrusted. Sometimes the light played a cruel trick and she could almost see the promise of whiskers starting to grow on his face. When that happened in earnest, she might not know him anymore.

"We're already trying to keep him from being alone with Mrs. Crowley," he said. "Can we keep him away from both of them?"

"Mrs. Crowley doesn't matter," Melanie said. "He doesn't seem to like her above half, for all that he tries to be polite. Did you see his face when she put her daughters on his lap last night? He was so surprised he almost dropped them. She even had the gall to say what a shame it is he never married, because he would make a wonderful father. Just as if he isn't a father to *us* already!"

After that, Mrs. Crowley had tried to shoo Melanie away when she had gone to Uncle Robert for a hug. Mrs. Crowley told her, right in front of Uncle Robert, that it was improper for a big girl like Melanie to sit on a gentleman's lap. Uncle Robert had scooped Melanie up and given Mrs. Crowley a brittle smile.

"I'm not just any gentleman," he had said, giving Mrs. Crowley a reproving look. "I'm her favorite uncle, isn't that true, Melanie, love?"

Mrs. Crowley had puffed all up like a toad and bit her lip when Melanie gave her a smug smile. It had felt *good*. Then the woman's lips wavered, and she got this big, insincere smile on her face and tried to laugh it off as a joke.

No. Mrs. Crowley wasn't the threat anymore.

It was Lady Madelyn.

She wouldn't have him, Melanie vowed. Not while there was breath left in Melanie's body.

Three

Lady Madelyn stood patiently while her maid unhurriedly tweaked her evening gown into more becoming lines.

It was really a delightful creation, if rather too dashing to be wasted on a country dinner party. One of her Paris gowns, it consisted of a half robe in sea-green gauze over a slip of amaranthus-purple crepe de chine. The robe was appliquéd at the shoulders in a pattern of amaranthus butterflies. Her mother's incomparable matched pearls surrounded her long, graceful neck, glimmered at her ears, and formed a bandeau to confine the loose curls swept up at the crown of her head.

When she wore this gown for the first time at an embassy reception, Count Andreas Briccetti couldn't seem to take his eyes off her. She had thought at the time she saw more in his eyes than simple admiration, but she obviously had been mistaken.

"Perfect," Bettina said, smiling.

"True," Madelyn said, giving an approving nod in the mirror her maid held for her. "Do you miss the Continent, Bettina? A house party in the country is hardly scope for your talents."

"Not at all, my lady," Bettina said, looking surprised. "It is pleasant being below stairs with persons who speak proper English after all those years of being scared to death I was going to make a mistake and embarrass you in front of all your fine princes and diplomats and such. It gets wearing on a body to be grand all the time. Thank you kindly for asking."

Madelyn realized that this was the first time she had asked the maid such a personal question in the two years she had served her. Bettina had been a fresh-faced, ambitious girl eager to see the world when Madelyn hired her with only a cursory examination of her scanty references just before she left England to crisscross the Continent. Madelyn's former dresser of many years had been highly skilled and London bred; she refused to follow her mistress to foreign parts. Madelyn had been desperate to engage a substitute in a hurry before her ship left for France. What Bettina had lacked in skill, she made up for in a refreshing enthusiasm and eagerness to please. Madelyn had given no thought at all to what those years had been like for Bettina as the girl made herself indispensable to her. Had she thought her maid just ceased to exist when she had no use for her?

"Bettina, where are your people?" she asked. "You have not seen them in all the years we have been gone, have you?"

Madelyn didn't miss the sheen of tears that sprang to her maid's eyes. The girl looked embarrassed.

"Wiltshire," she said wistfully. "My younger sisters and brothers will have forgotten me, I fear."

Bettina gave Madelyn a brave smile.

"Forgive me, my lady, for going on like that. It must be all the children in the house. Will there be anything else?"

"No, Bettina," she started to say; then she changed her mind. "Yes, Bettina. Would you like to leave for

Wiltshire tomorrow to spend Christmas with your family?"

Bettina's mouth dropped open.

"My lady!" she said with a girlish squeal of delight. "You're not meaning it!"

"Certainly, I am, er, do. I can get along without you for a little while. Lady Letitia's dresser can do for me as well while I am here, if she does not mind. I will speak to Lady Letitia about it."

"I would be ever so grateful," Bettina said. "Being here and seeing all the children about has made me homesick, but I never would have mentioned it, as I hope you know, my lady."

"I know," Madelyn said, feeling like an ogre for not making arrangements for Bettina to visit her family sooner. If Lady Letitia minded sharing her dresser with her, Madelyn decided, she would manage somehow on her own. How difficult could it be?

"I will never forget your kindness, ma'am!" Bettina said.

"Pray, do not regard it," Madelyn said. It was a small enough boon, after all. "You might start packing your belongings tonight so you can be ready to leave in the morning."

Madelyn left Bettina almost incoherent with gratitude and still had a little smile of satisfaction on her face when she walked out of her room and came face-to-face with Robert Langtry in the corridor.

"Robert!" she exclaimed, startled. "Or Mr. Langtry, I should say."

"Robert, please," he said. His eyes were warm with admiration as they rested on the magnificence of her appearance. "You are quite dazzling tonight."

"Mr. Langtry," Madelyn said firmly. She hoped the exasperating man did not think she was dressing up to impress *him!* "Visiting your flirt, Mrs. Crowley, are you?"

Why, she scolded herself, *did I say that? It sounded as if I am jealous.* Which was true, but *he* wasn't to know that.

"Hardly," he said with a laugh. "She is my mother's friend, not mine."

Madelyn merely lifted her eyebrows at him. He couldn't be *that* dense.

"Actually," Robert continued, "I was about to see if Melanie and Mark were prepared for dinner. They are considered grown-up enough to join the adults now. Or at least they are by Lady Blakely's standards. She always includes her younger sisters at dinner, so we decided it would be unfair not to include my children as well."

My children.

He said it so easily. One could tell by the way his eyes laughed when he was around his wards that he loved them dearly. She hoped his wards knew how lucky they were. Her own parents, like the governesses, teachers, and guardian who followed them, considered being with her more a duty than a source of affection and pleasure.

Madelyn gave herself an impatient mental shake. What business did *she* have to feel sorry for herself? She was rich. She was beautiful, if her admirers and her own mirror were to be believed. She had everything but . . . him.

"Would you like to accompany me?"

"I beg your pardon?" she asked.

"To visit the children."

"No. I thank you," she said, amazed that he would suggest such a thing. Surprise made her blunt. "Children make me uncomfortable. You should know that by now, Mr. Langtry."

"As you please," he said a bit stiffly. "I will see you at dinner."

Up ahead, a door opened.

"Uncle Robert!" his younger nephew called out. "Are you quite sure I am not old enough to go to dinner with you?"

"Quite sure, my lad," Robert said. "None of your pouting, my girl," he added jovially to Mary as she appeared behind her brother with lower lip out-thrust. The girl brightened when she saw Madelyn.

"Good evening, Lady Madelyn," she called out. Madelyn couldn't help smiling at the child in her white nightgown. She looked so sweet, like a little blond angel.

"You wore it, just like you promised!" Mary said ecstatically as she ran to Madelyn and walked all the way around her to admire her gown. "Lady Madelyn promised she would wear it just for me tonight when I visited her in her room today and chose it for her," the child added for Robert's benefit when he raised one eyebrow in inquiry.

"Children make you uncomfortable, do they?" he murmured, not quite under his breath.

Conscious of Robert's amused gaze upon her, Madelyn swept Mary a formal curtsy, and the girl clapped her hands in pleasure. Mary then took the skirt of her nightgown in one hand and made an answering curtsy with her back as straight as a young poplar, just the way Madelyn had taught her. Madelyn felt a curious sense of pride in the child's performance.

Mary obediently took Robert's outstretched hand, and they started walking toward the open door. Then Robert turned and solemnly extended his other hand to Madelyn in invitation.

Madelyn hesitated on the verge of following him

and Mary, after all. Light spilled out from the open door into the corridor, surrounding Robert, Mary, and Matthew in a warm glow. Madelyn was drawn to that warmth as a moth is to a flame.

But it was not for her, she told herself firmly.

It would never be for her.

Madelyn smiled and shook her head. Robert's smile faded as he gave a careless shrug of his shoulders and guided Mary and Matthew back inside the room, closing the door behind them.

He didn't look back at her.

Madelyn considered the closed door for a moment, then straightened her spine and made her solitary way to the drawing room.

"I don't know why these things keep falling down," huffed Lydia Whittaker as she stood on a chair, reattaching a sprig of mistletoe to the kissing bough in the center of the ceiling.

Madelyn gasped, for Lydia was rosily pregnant, and although Madelyn was hardly a judge of such things, she had a strong suspicion that Lydia should not have been indulging in such an athletic activity so close to her lying-in. This opinion was loudly confirmed by the lady's husband, Lt. Edward Whittaker, when he walked into the room behind Madelyn.

"Lydia!" he bellowed. "Have you taken leave of your senses? What in the name of heaven do you think you are doing?"

A member of the Prince Regent's Own Tenth Royal Hussars, the blond, blue-eyed officer was an imposing figure in his dress uniform of blue with gold lacing. Normally he was the soul of good-natured calm, but marriage to his Lydia apparently had changed all that.

He stalked over to the chair, grasped his wife by the waist, and set her on the floor. Then he kissed her as if he had just rescued her from deadly peril.

Embarrassed and, if the truth be known, a bit envious, Madelyn averted her eyes to give them privacy.

Until now it had not occurred to Madelyn that it might be awkward to attend a house party containing not one, not two, but *three* of her former suitors under one roof. In truth, Lord Blakely never had officially offered for her, but the likelihood of their marriage was assumed by the *tôn* for years. When he married Vanessa Whittaker instead and Madelyn's passion for Robert Langtry seemed hopeless, Madelyn thought Edward Whittaker, the scion of the rich branch of the Whittaker family, might do as well. Certainly his parents and her guardian had led her to believe that marriage to her was his most ardent desire. Then he fell madly in love with plain, squabbish little Lydia Whittaker, and once again Madelyn was an object of pity and scorn by all the gossips.

At least Robert had done her the very great favor of not falling in love with another woman in such indecent haste! It was some consolation, but not much. She had loved him with all her heart.

"Oh, Lady Madelyn," said the radiantly smiling Lydia when she emerged from her husband's crushing embrace. "I did not see you there."

Madelyn told herself she was probably imagining Lydia's smug look, the one that said, *You may be rich—your gown may have come straight from Paris—but I snatched this outrageously handsome man right out from under your aristocratic nose and I am thrice the woman you will ever be because I am having his child, so there!*

"Lady Madelyn," said Lieutenant Whittaker, smiling rather absently at her as he tucked his round, little wife into the crook of his arm. "How charming you look! I see your travels have not diminished your beauty in the slightest."

It was rather difficult to take this seriously when he was obviously so preoccupied with his wife, but the compliment soothed Madelyn's rapidly deteriorating sense of self-esteem and smoothed over the moment of awkwardness.

"Now, my dear," the lieutenant said, turning away from Madelyn with unflattering haste to Lydia. "What possessed you to get up on a chair when you are increasing?"

"The mistletoe somehow came loose, so I was merely tacking it up again. And I will just mention, Edward, that it is excessively improper to bandy about my condition in public like that! What will Lady Madelyn think?"

"What? Is it a secret?" he joked, giving his wife's plump shoulders an affectionate squeeze and placing a fleeting touch on her rounded stomach. She blushed and slapped his hand away.

Madelyn had to laugh at this somewhat improper teasing. She exchanged polite commonplaces with them until they moved toward one of the sofas. Then she strolled to the velvet-cushioned window seat to look out into the night. The moon was full, and she could see the large, lacy flakes of snow glisten against it as they fell to earth to join the pristine blanket already covering Lord Blakely's grounds. Madelyn resolved to get up early for a ride on horseback. Lord Blakely, who owned some of the finest horseflesh in the county, would have a number of fine mounts available for the use of his guests. Madelyn had packed two riding habits in anticipation.

While she was lost in these musings, she felt a tentative touch on her shoulder and turned to stare into Robert Langtry's laughing eyes. Incredibly, he brushed her lips with the lightest and sweetest of kisses.

"My apologies," he said, smiling at her. "I couldn't resist."

To her look of bemused inquiry, he pointed upward, and she saw the sprig of mistletoe suspended in the upper frame of the window seat.

His smile faded, and his eyes searched hers.

She had to say something.

Now.

"The silly things seem to be all over the house," she said inanely.

"One may only hope," he murmured, giving her a wicked grin.

Then he turned away from her as if the kiss were nothing of import, a mere concession to custom.

What else, she scolded herself, *could it be but a kiss between old friends?*

Melanie, his niece, had stopped just inside the door and was staring at Madelyn with a look so malevolent that Madelyn was surprised she didn't burst into flames. Mark merely looked embarrassed.

"Ah, I see a gentleman standing under the mistletoe," Madelyn said in a valiant attempt to lighten the atmosphere. Mark looked around to see whom she meant, and his eyes widened as she advanced upon him. He was standing squarely beneath the kissing bough. He blushed endearingly when she kissed him softly on the cheek.

Robert laughed in amusement, but his dark-haired niece merely looked disgusted.

Madelyn's heart suddenly broke with pity for Melanie. She remembered that age, and she wouldn't relive it for all the diamonds in Africa. She learned when she was very young to bury her anger deep inside, for to do otherwise would be to invite punishment. Melanie, however, had a loving uncle, so she never had been forced to adopt such subterfuge.

"Melanie!" exclaimed Mrs. Crowley with a disapproving titter, entering the room with Mrs. Langtry. "What a face! You'll quite frighten Lady Madelyn!"

Mrs. Langtry gave an answering titter in appreciation of what apparently passed as wit in bucolic circles and put a hand on her granddaughter's shoulder.

Melanie merely scowled, which made her nose look longer.

Fortunately, at that moment their hostess's younger sisters, Amy and Aggie, entered the room on each side of their mother. They raced at once to Melanie's side and took her away with them to the now-vacant window seat where their giggling confidences swept Melanie's ill humor away. Robert, of course, had to exclaim over the fact that three beauties were coyly residing under the mistletoe and give each one a loud, smacking kiss on the cheek.

Their hostess's mother swept a knowledgeable eye over Madelyn's gown when she found herself standing beside her.

"That shade of sea green is so lovely with your coloring, Lady Madelyn," Mrs. Annabelle Whittaker said almost grudgingly. She never had liked Madelyn, for she once considered her a threat to Lydia's happiness.

"Yes, it makes your hair look so . . . bright," said Mrs. Crowley in an overloud voice.

Madelyn lifted her eyebrows, for this was unmistakably a declaration of war, implying, of course, that Madelyn's hair was a vulgar color. Mrs. Crowley's complexion was heightened, and her eyes were bright with malice. Still, her lips were smiling, and once again Madelyn was repelled by the combination.

If you're going to insult someone, Madelyn's father had always said, at least be honest about it. Planting the barb and trying to pretend it was not intentional was a coward's stratagem.

"Thank you," Madelyn said, refusing to retaliate in kind. That would be to acknowledge some sort of competition between them, and Madelyn would not dignify the lady's pretensions by doing so.

If Robert Langtry was stupid enough to marry this harpy, he could do so with Madelyn's very goodwill!

Mr. Wyndham appeared in the doorway, and Madelyn surreptitiously moved as far away from the kissing bough as possible. She had no intention of providing entertainment for this ill-assorted group by enduring Mr. Wyndham's kiss.

Not while her lips still tingled pleasantly from Robert's.

She thought she had performed this maneuver unobtrusively enough until she felt Robert's eyes on her. She glanced at him, and those eyes were laughing at her.

So much for subtlety.

Mrs. Langtry pushed Mrs. Crowley under the mistletoe and cleared her throat with a meaningful look at her son, but he suddenly became engrossed in a conversation with Lydia and Edward and could pretend he did not see her. Madelyn's spirits lifted a little at this.

Mr. Wyndham had no choice, then, but to kiss Mrs. Crowley, which he did with apparent willingness. Then he came to stand beside Madelyn.

"Hardly the most elegant of company, is it?" he said humorously, although she could tell he was displeased. He expected her to commiserate with him, for dining with a handful of giggling adolescents, tittering dowagers, and a female who looked capable of dropping a full-term child at the least provocation wasn't quite what she was accustomed to, either.

"I have known our hosts and the Whittakers for years," she said, perversely refusing to gratify him. It was against her principles to accept a couple's hospitality and then disparage their arrangements under their own roof. Mr. Wyndham's willingness to do so was yet another unattractive trait.

Mr. Wyndham frowned, but he turned to smile eagerly at the Earl of Stoneham and Lady Letitia when they swept into the room with their host and hostess. Even the most top-lofty snob, Madelyn reflected cynically, could not object to the company of an earl.

Vanessa was all apologies.

"I beg your pardon," she said prettily. "We were visiting the boys in the nursery, and they would *not* settle down! Do let us go into dinner."

Dinner was rather a noisier meal than those to which Madelyn was accustomed. For one thing, she quickly learned that her hosts did not believe in the old adage that children should be seen and not heard.

The younger Whittaker girls cajoled sweetly for a sleigh ride in the moonlight, and their mother insisted the night air would be extremely injurious to their health. Their elder sister, Lydia, agreed with her, but Aggie pointed out with some heat that Lydia was just jealous because Edward would not let *her* go because of her condition.

Since "the condition" was something proper young ladies and gentlemen did not acknowledge in public—not even when the proof of it was so conspicuous that one could hardly be unaware of it—the girl's mother looked as if she might have an attack of the vapors from pure embarrassment. She and Mrs. Langtry exchanged a look of commiseration when Melanie and Mark loudly seconded Amy and Aggie's suggestion.

"It didn't hurt us last night when Alexander took us out," Aggie said with an exaggerated pout.

"Alexander!" exclaimed Vanessa, turning incredulous eyes on her husband. *"That's* where you were when I thought you were out smoking one of your horrid cigars."

Alexander had the grace to look sheepish.

"It was such a beautiful evening," he said. Madelyn had to smile. Alexander was an officer in the late war and had been decorated by Wellington himself for bravery. But he positively quailed under his wife's gaze.

"Alexander made sure Nurse bundled James and Jeremy up quite warmly, I promise you," Aggie interjected in an unfortunate attempt to absolve her brother-in-law from blame.

"You took my babies out in this weather *at night?*" Vanessa cried. Alexander winced and hung his head.

She turned to Robert, who was trying very hard not to laugh.

"And I suppose," she said forbiddingly, "that *you* were a party to this, Robert."

"Guilty," he said, unrepentant. "We all enjoyed it excessively. Now that the whole affair is out in the open, you can go with us tonight."

"Men," Vanessa said in accents of loathing at this audacity, but her lips were twitching.

"Think how boring your life would be without us," the lieutenant suggested. "I must say, I am quite offended that you didn't invite me to go along," he added.

"I wanted to tell you, Edward," Alexander admitted, "but Robert insisted you would only tell Lydia and then the fat *would* be in the fire!"

"I see you have decided between you all that my wife rules the roost in my family," said Edward with some asperity.

"Of course, darling," Lydia said audaciously. "Have I not always said you were the most sensible of men? If you think it would be quite safe, perhaps I shall go, after all."

"Lydia!" gasped Edward. "Under no circumstances will you go! I *forbid* it."

"Let's see," Lydia said, ignoring him. "I think we probably will need two sleighs and a great quantity of blankets."

"Lydia, you are *not* going!" her husband interjected.

"Oh, *do* calm down, Edward," she said. "If there are two sleighs, one of them can contain us and the children so we may turn back after only half an hour or so. The others may proceed to ruin their health to their heart's content."

"That does seem sensible," Vanessa said thoughtfully. "That would mean Edward and Lydia and I will go in the large sleigh with the twins, Aggie and Amy, Mark, Melanie, Mary and Matthew, Laura and Aimée—"

"My daughters will *not* be a party to any such scheme!" asserted Mrs. Crowley in disapproval. "What can you be thinking, Lady Blakely, to permit such a thing?"

"As you wish," Vanessa said coolly. "Then that would leave Edward, Lydia, Mark, Melanie, Mary and Matthew, and Aggie and Amy in our sleigh—"

At this point, all the young people began to complain loudly at being consigned to the shorter excursion.

Mrs. Crowley and Mr. Wyndham both looked appalled by such bad manners at table and exchanged incredulous looks.

"We don't want to ride with the babies," sulked Melanie. Aggie and Amy nodded emphatically.

"I say, Uncle Robert, why can I not ride with you and the other men?" Mark objected. "I shall be going to University in—"

"Because we need another man to accompany the ladies and children," Robert said in a conspiratorial voice. "I know I can count on you to help Lieutenant Whittaker keep them safe."

"Oh, in that case, then—" the youth said, restored to good humor.

"But what about us?" Melanie persisted.

"Melanie, it has been decided," Robert told her with an understanding smile. "Perhaps, if all goes well, you can go on a longer ride tomorrow during the day."

"Lady Madelyn," Mr. Wyndham whispered in a voice that carried quite clearly to the other diners. "I hope *you* are not going to lend yourself to this outrageous scheme."

"A sleigh ride in the moonlight sounds exciting," she said. "I would not miss it for the world. Will you not come with us, Lord Stoneham?"

"I should be delighted," that gentleman declared with a twinkle in his eye, as Madelyn knew he would. The earl considered it a source of great pride that he was as hale and hearty as men thirty years his junior.

"And I hope *you* will ride in the second carriage with those of us who intend to stay out later, my dear," the earl added. "It has been too long since we went adventuring together."

"Certainly, for it sounds as if the other sleigh will be quite a squeeze," Madelyn agreed.

"Very well, I shall go, too," said Mr. Wyndham, apparently determined to prevent Madelyn from being the sole female occupant in a sleigh with three gentlemen.

"And I, also," Mrs. Crowley added, no doubt for the same reason.

"Lovely! Then it is settled," said Alexander, beaming. "Vanessa will come with us, of course. Lydia, Aggie and Amy can take charge of the boys for such a short time."

"Of course, darling, if you wish it," his wife said, giving him an adoring smile.

They retired to their rooms for warm clothing and then emerged from the nursery with their arms full of excited children bundled to the eyes in blankets and heavy mufflers.

Madelyn's blood hummed in her veins at the prospect of such an adventure.

Robert's eyes gleamed as he handed her into the sleigh. Before he could get in beside her, Mrs. Crowley practically knocked him down so she could insinuate herself next to Madelyn and thus be wedged between them. Grumbling, Mr. Wyndham sat in the less desirable forward seat. He brightened when Lord Stoneham sat next to him, but the earl gave the younger man a discouraging glance when Mr. Wyndham was obviously about to embark upon a session of serious toad-eating. Although Mr. Wyndham was a prime favorite with Lady Letitia, the earl obviously was unimpressed by him.

"Madelyn, my dear," the earl said imperiously.

"After enticing me along on this ride, the least you can do is sit beside me."

"With pleasure," she replied with alacrity, not looking forward to the prospect of sitting next to Mrs. Crowley. The woman had given Madelyn such a poisonous look at dinner that it was surprising Madelyn did not fall dead on the spot. This left Alexander as driver, Lord Stoneham, Madelyn, and Mr. Wyndham in the forward seat, and Robert and Mrs. Crowley facing them. Madelyn smiled at the squeals of excitement coming from the other sleigh. Vanessa, after giving her sisters detailed instructions about the care of her sons, slipped in beside Mrs. Crowley.

It took so long for everyone to get settled in the other sleigh that Madelyn, wearing a sable-lined, hooded cloak she had purchased in Russia and sandwiched tightly between the two men, was so warm she almost nodded off. Then she heard Alexander give a shout of sheer exhilaration as he started the horses forward. The brisk wind revived Madelyn with a slap of drifting snow against her face.

"It is so beautiful!" she exclaimed as the earl smiled down into her upturned face.

"I used to take you and Alexander out in our sleigh when you were a little girl, Madelyn, do you remember?" he said, giving her hand an affectionate squeeze.

"Very well," she said, grinning at him. "It is the happiest memory of my childhood. Oh, I love the snow! Isn't it wonderful?"

Vanessa and Mrs. Crowley were looking at her in surprise, as if they doubted she even *had* a childhood.

"Yes," said Mrs. Crowley as she shivered and burrowed into her coat. "It is quite refreshing, is it not, after being confined indoors within those warm rooms?"

She said this last a bit longingly.

No doubt with the intention of helping Cupid in his mission to lure Robert to the altar, Vanessa deliberately crowded Mrs. Crowley so she would be squashed in close to Robert. The merest civility obliged him to put his arm along the back of the sleigh to give the ladies more room. This, of course, positioned Mrs. Crowley practically in his arms. Madelyn managed to refrain from childishly baring her teeth at Mrs. Crowley's triumphant smirk in her direction.

"I say, let's have a song!" Robert suggested gleefully. "We happen to have aboard our sleigh a lady whose soprano is so clear and so fine that she has been compared to—"

"Madame Catalani, I know," said Madelyn, rolling her eyes. "I suppose you are never going to leave off teasing me about that flight of fancy on the part of some imaginative wag who had the ill-conceived inspiration to bandy it about in the newspapers."

"The Prince Regent himself appeared to agree with the fellow, whoever he was," Robert said.

"I did not know you were so fond of the society columns, Mr. Langtry," Madelyn said archly. He looked a bit embarrassed, so she relented. "My singing master used to warn me that I would ruin my voice if I went out in the night air and, above all, if I would *sing* out-of-doors. Let us by all means put his theory to the test. If we all sound like frogs tomorrow morning, we will know whom to blame, Mr. Langtry."

"You must not sing on any account if you think it will be injurious to your voice," Robert said, looking troubled.

"I was merely teasing, Mr. Langtry," Madelyn said

gently. "I assure you I have put my voice to the test many times and taken no harm from it."

"She can bellow like a moose at full charge at all hours without a croak the next morning!" Alexander called cheerfully from his perch.

Madelyn turned around to bat him playfully on the back, and her cloak started to slip. She repressed an impulse to roll her eyes at the way Mr. Wyndham's hands lingered at her shoulders when he caught up the cloak and solicitously settled it back around her. His apparent assumption of some understanding between them was extremely vexing, for she had promised him *nothing*.

"What shall we sing?" she asked the earl, unobtrusively leaning toward Lord Stoneham so Mr. Wyndham's body would no longer be brushing hers. "Something French? Something Italian?"

"Let's have a song in good English, Lady Madelyn," Robert said. "Something merry so we can all join in."

"Merry," repeated Madelyn thoughtfully.

She threw back her head and started singing. "On the first day of Christmas, my true love gave to me . . ."

"A partridge in a pear tree . . ." warbled Robert, Alexander and Vanessa exuberantly.

Four

Robert stepped out into the chill air of the morning and watched his breath expel puffs of white vapor against the pink-tinged blue of the dawning sky. It was so lovely it made his heart ache.

Like Lady Madelyn.

His mind had been filled with the purity of her singing as he sat in the sleigh, burning for her.

She was as far above him as the angels in heaven.

He felt a little guilty for deliberately sneaking out of the house so early to discourage his wards from accompanying him. Ordinarily there was nothing he enjoyed more than exploring the countryside with the children, but this morning he needed a little peace. He also had no wish to have Mrs. Crowley fussing over him.

Poor woman. She thought the way to his heart was through proving to him that he needed a woman to take charge of his wards. Her disparaging remarks about how he was rearing them cut to the bone. No, they weren't perfect, but they were his flesh and blood. He spoiled them, she insisted with a superior smile, as if nothing else could be expected of a mere man. On the contrary, he could never do enough for them. They were all he had left of his only brother. How he wished he had told John he loved him while he was still alive, for all that his brother would have stared at such mawkish sentimentality.

Mrs. Crowley, not to be undone by Madelyn, had sung last night, too. They all had. But Mrs. Crowley was just a little louder than the others, and not precisely on key. She had led the chorus many times at her husband's church and prided herself on her taste and ability to organize a jumble of voices into harmony. After Madelyn's song, she proceeded to divide everyone into parts and lead them in the singing herself. Lord Stoneham merely gave her a cool stare and declined to accept a part. Mr. Wyndham looked as if he would have liked to follow suit, but Madelyn caught his eye and gave him a wry little smile, so he reluctantly allowed Mrs. Crowley to tell him when and what to sing. Not that Mrs. Crowley cared what the earl, Mr. Wyndham, or Madelyn thought. Her eyes were on Robert the whole time, as if for approval. She would show him that she knew more than some society ornament like Lady Madelyn about singing, by heaven!

Robert felt like a rag being savaged between two dogs, although neither lady would thank him for the comparison.

Mrs. Crowley was such a capable woman. There was a rough kindness beneath her officious exterior that was quite attractive, but Robert could think of nothing worse than to be shackled to her for life.

This morning she would be bustling about the house, getting in Vanessa's housekeeper's way with her suggestions for greater economy or efficiency, and she would have her children up and dressed and doing lessons at her knee while all the other lady guests were still in bed, drinking their chocolate and eating sweet biscuits as they contemplated their toilettes for the afternoon's activities.

But, no, Robert realized as he looked up at the door to the house. There was Lady Madelyn dressed in a black riding habit that set off her porcelain skin and bright hair to perfection. A jaunty little hat was set at an angle on her elegant head, and her maid was with her. The servant carried a small traveling case.

Puzzled, Robert approached them.

"May I be of assistance?" Robert asked.

"Not unless you would like to drive Bettina into Wiltshire," Madelyn said pleasantly. "Were you going for a ride, Mr. Langtry? If so, perhaps you will be kind enough to wait for me to join you. I shall be ready as soon as I see Bettina off. Ah, here we are."

To Robert's surprise, a gig was approaching from the stables.

"Here is money for the journey, Bettina," Madelyn said, taking the girl's hand and placing a small purse into it. "Enjoy yourself, but take care to present yourself at my cousin's house as soon as the holiday is over. You know I cannot do without you for very long."

"Yes, my lady," the girl said tearfully. "Thank you, my lady! I can never thank you enough."

"You have thanked me quite sufficiently for so trifling a favor, Bettina," she said kindly. "Go now! You want to arrive at the inn before the stagecoach leaves!"

The driver of the gig extended his hand and pulled the girl into the seat beside him. She looked back once, and Madelyn waved reassuringly at her. Smiling, she waved back.

"There," said Madelyn with satisfaction as she gave Robert a dazzling smile. "Now for a gallop in the snow!"

"Where is your maid going?" Robert asked. "Has there been a death in her family?"

"No. On the contrary, Bettina is going to spend Christmas with her family in Wiltshire for the first time in two years. She will join me after the holiday in Yorkshire, for I am to go to my cousin's house for New Year's."

"To Yorkshire," he said stupidly. Lady Madelyn was going to Yorkshire? "May I offer you a place in our carriage?"

"That is excessively kind, but I have brought my own traveling coach, thank you," she said. "Even at that, it will be a tight squeeze with all of my clothes."

Of course. Lady Madelyn would travel post at the greatest possible speed with her own coach and driver. Robert, his mother, and the children would travel by easy stages, spending the night in inns along the way and resting his own horses so that there would be no need to change them. He had learned early in his guardianship that children became excessively cranky after several days on the road, with thirty-minute stops at a time for meals.

"You are not afraid to go alone?" he asked.

"Certainly not," she said. "I have traveled all over the Continent with only Bettina for company. I venture to think I can travel in my own country safely with my own coachman and guard."

What a lonely life, Robert thought, pitying her, for all that she would stare to hear him say so.

She probably would call it freedom.

"Alexander has this lovely mare in his stable, the dove-gray one with the black markings," Lady Madelyn was saying. "That is the one I want. Now we only have to see what is available for you."

Once in the stables, Madelyn selected a sidesaddle and waited for a groom to put it on her chosen horse

while another groom led out a spirited black stallion
for Robert. It was not Lord Blakely's personal mount,
much as Robert would have enjoyed testing Midnight's mettle, but Robert knew Alexander's Midnight was capable of throwing him off before he had
traveled ten paces down the road, and he wasn't
about to risk looking like a clumsy fool in front of
Lady Madelyn.

They had just mounted the horses when Mr. Wyndham came running, winded, into the stables.

"Lady Madelyn!" he puffed. "If you will wait a moment, I will accompany you."

He gave Robert a poisonous look. Obviously the
man had dressed in a hurry and rushed out into the
cold morning in hopes of a tête-à-tête with Madelyn.

"You can catch up with us, Mr. Wyndham," Madelyn said as she turned her horse away from him and
set off at a slow walk out of the stable. Robert tried
to stifle a triumphant smile as he followed her.

"I should not be surprised if Mrs. Crowley appears
as well, shivering and ill-tempered but determined
to keep you out of my evil clutches," she said with
some asperity when they were out in the yard.

"I doubt if she would be so foolish," Robert said
mildly. He *wished* he was in danger of being pursued
by Lady Madelyn. "The surrounding woods are probably denuded of mistletoe in the interests of bringing
you and Mr. Wyndham, and me and Pamela Crowley,
to the altar."

"We are perfectly sensible adults capable of leading our own lives without all these interfering busy-
bodies to drive us to distraction," Madelyn groused.
"Do I need a man? No! I have a handsome fortune.
I am invited everywhere in society. I have a perfectly
charming life!"

"Indeed," Robert said, depressingly aware that her

life wouldn't be nearly so charming if she had succeeded in convincing him to elope with her two years ago.

"Yet my godmother is tireless in her efforts to marry me off to various tedious creatures. My head would be quite turned by all the suitors I have had underfoot if I did not know perfectly well they were only interested in my fortune."

"Not all of them, surely," Robert said.

Madelyn gave him a long look.

"All of them," she insisted, and galloped away so suddenly that Robert was caught unaware. It took him some time to catch up with her as she raced like a madwoman along the road, laughing as her horse's hooves kicked up clouds of snow at the drifted parts of the track.

Something about the reckless sound of that laughter gave him chills.

"Madelyn! What is *wrong* with you!" he shouted when he caught up with her and she slowed the horse to a walk. They had entered the woods, and the dense growth of trees made it dangerous to proceed with any speed.

"Nothing!" she insisted, abruptly swinging off the horse before he could assist her. She sat down on a large rock, careless of the toll such rash action might take on her expensive riding habit. Robert tied the horses to a tree off the track, then cringed and sat down next to her. Could she not feel how *cold* that rock was through her clothes? Of course, she had all those voluminous skirts to protect her from frostbite; a gentleman's pantaloons were not nearly so accommodating in that regard.

She gave a brittle laugh.

"Me! With a husband and children! Can you imagine anything more ridiculous?" she said mockingly.

"Many things," Robert said, trying to keep his voice even.

She shoved him away and sat straighter, adopting a heartbreakingly tough voice.

"Children don't even like me," she asserted, sounding very much like Melanie when she said she didn't *care* that Mary was pretty and she wasn't. Who needed to be pretty, anyway? "And I don't like them."

"Is that why you let Mary keep the green hat?" he asked, trying hard not to smile.

"That was nothing," she said with a negligent wave of her hand. "I would have given it to my maid in a week or so. The plume was not even worth replacing."

"Lydia says it has Paris written all over it," Robert said.

"Well! When Lydia Whittaker becomes an arbiter of fashion, pigs may fly! And I will thank you not to discuss my personal affairs with any of those provoking Whittakers!"

"Mary likes you."

"Only because I gave her the hat. That's the only reason people like rich people—because they give them things."

"That is not true. You remind her of her mother, and there was not a kinder woman alive than Eleanor."

"Mary likes to look at my gowns. That is not the same as liking someone. Anyway, the other children don't like me. Except maybe for the fat little boy."

"Matthew? He likes everyone."

"There. You see?"

"I see that you are properly blue-deviled, my dear." He looked up to see a horseman riding toward them. "Blast! Here is your second-most-ardent admirer now."

"Second-most?"

"I am your most ardent," Robert said, proud of the way he made it come out like a joke. "Always."

Robert quickly took her hand and pulled her to her feet, propelling them both into a pile of drifting snow behind the rock. Leaning above her, he put a hand over her mouth to stifle her startled scream. Fortunately, the horses were not quite visible from the track unless one was unusually observant.

Sure enough, Mr. Wyndham kept right on going. Robert risked a look over the top of the rock at him as he passed by, and to Robert's unworthy satisfaction, the man's well-bred, aquiline nose was red with cold. His shivering posture made him look positively inept in the saddle.

When Mr. Wyndham took a bend in the track and was out of sight, Robert removed his hand from Madelyn's mouth. Before she could give voice to her indignation, he bent his head and kissed her.

She is going to slap you until your ears ring, he told himself, but he didn't care. To his gratification, she kissed him back, quite thoroughly.

Then she slapped him.

"I deserved that," he said, although he was not in the least repentant.

"You certainly did. Another hat ruined!" She complained. She deliberately avoided looking at his face. "We shall have to tell them I took a tumble, I suppose."

Robert stood and offered his hand. She ignored it and got to her feet unassisted.

"I'll get the horses," Robert said meekly. What could have possessed him? She had confided in him, like a friend, and he had forced himself on her.

"Robert."

He turned back, and she touched his cheek with one gentle gloved finger. The smell of supple Spanish leather, blended with her perfume, made his senses swim.

You've got it bad, old man, he admitted to himself.

"We shall have to tell them you got whipped in the face by a branch," she said apologetically. "You can see the imprint of my fingers on your face."

Robert was such a lovesick fool, he hoped he was marked by her touch forever.

"I deserved that," he said again.

Incredibly, she smiled at him.

"Maybe *I'm* the one who deserves to be slapped for whining about my cruel fate on such a beautiful day," she said, taking his arm. "Now let's go for that ride. Suddenly, I feel so alive!"

So did Robert, heaven help him!

"I do not understand why the mistletoe keeps falling down," Lydia complained. Her husband caught her arm when she would have dragged a chair over to repair the damage.

"This, my darling, is why clever, petite ladies marry tall men," he told her as he took the sprig of mistletoe from her hand and reached up to attach it to the end of the kissing bough quite easily.

"You were always a show-off," she said, trying without success to look disgruntled. "I made sure it was attached quite securely the last time it fell down."

"My love, has it occurred to you that perhaps some members of this party are not so anxious to aid Cupid in marrying off Robert Langtry to Mrs. Crowley as you are?"

She thought for a moment and then gave a startled exclamation.

"The children, of course! Melanie is not quite tall enough, but she is certainly capable of dragging a chair over as I did. And Mark would probably help her, just for the joy of playing a prank. Well!"

She folded her arms over her expanding middle and looked adorably like a ruffled little hen. Edward couldn't resist dropping a kiss on the top of her head.

"One can hardly blame them," he said. "The prospect of having a monument to organization like Mrs. Crowley as their guardian's wife would make even the most angelic children resort to mutiny. And the perfect manners of her unnaturally well behaved daughters would inspire any normal child to thoughts of mayhem."

"Pamela Crowley is a very worthy woman!" Lydia insisted. "She is *exactly* what Robert needs."

"But she isn't what Robert *wants,*" Edward said gently. "Do you not remember how little we appreciated our nearest and dearest trying to force us into marriages with persons they thought were exactly what we needed? If they had succeeded, *you* would have been married to Robert Langtry. And I, heaven help me, would have been married to Lady Madelyn."

He gave a theatrical shudder.

"I would have gone to my grave a miserable man," he added, kissing his wife on her tender little mouth.

"*Really,* darling?" she asked, her eyes alight with pleasure.

"*Really,* you sentimental little baggage," he said fondly. "Now, do stop fishing for compliments and go into breakfast. You must keep your strength up."

"Gladly," she said, tucking her hand into his arm.

"I must say this obsession everyone has with making me eat is quite refreshing after years of being nagged to go on various reducing diets."

She stopped and called out sharply.

"Melanie and Aggie!" she rapped out when the two girls emerged prematurely from their hiding places and then tried to duck back out of sight. At Lydia's summons they reluctantly stepped into the open. Melanie had a telltale sprig of greenery caught in her hair. "I think we have solved the mystery of the fallen mistletoe!"

"Don't scold, Lydia," Aggie said audaciously. "You know it is bad for you to be agitated."

"Vanessa was at such pains to decorate the house, and the two of you are undecorating it!"

"Besides," interjected Edward with a twinkle in his eye, "I believe you place a bit *too* much faith in the power of mistletoe to bring susceptible persons to the altar."

"See, Melanie," said Aggie. "I *told* you it would be more to the point to put a mouse in her bed."

"Aggie, for shame!" exclaimed Lydia. "Mrs. Crowley does not deserve to have such a mean trick played on her! How can you *think* of such a thing when she has so very kindly helped you rehearse the little entertainment you are planning to present to us tonight?"

"The mouse wasn't for Mrs. Crowley. *She* probably would give it a bath and teach it how to curtsy like stupid old Laura and Aimée," Melanie said bitterly. "It was for Lady Madelyn."

"If you do any such thing, I will be *extremely* put out with both of you, *and* I'll tell Mother and Robert, make no mistake!"

"Why?" Melanie asked, curious. "You don't like her, either. Grandmother said she almost stole Edward from you, and she was surprised you didn't tear her hair out by the roots.''

"From the mouths of babes,'' murmured Edward sotto voce.

"That was a long time ago,'' Lydia said, giving her husband a quelling look when he tried without success to keep a straight face. "Edward! You are *not* to encourage the little hoyden to bear tales!''

"Would you really have done it? Torn Lady Madelyn's hair out by the roots?'' he asked.

"Yes! And I fancy I would have found them brown instead of red!''

Everyone laughed heartily until Lydia looked up at the doorway and gasped. Lady Madelyn and Robert obviously had heard every word.

"Good morning,'' Robert said coldly, clenching his jaw. His look at Lydia made her blush crimson. Edward put a protective arm around his wife and gave Robert a belligerent stare.

Lady Madelyn, however, merely stripped off her riding gloves and gave the company a general nod of greeting.

"Lady Madelyn, I do apologize for my thoughtless remark,'' Lydia said.

Madelyn ignored her as if she had not spoken.

"Well, Mr. Langtry,'' she said. "I declare I am famished. Let us see if Lydia has left us anything to eat.''

She stared ostentatiously at Lydia's greatly expanded girth and strolled into the dining room.

"Well!'' huffed Lydia, insulted, as her husband patted her hand in sympathy. He knew that Lydia was sensitive about her weight despite her cheerful assertion that presenting a fashionable appearance didn't matter to her in the least.

"I have half a mind—'' Edward began as he glared after Madelyn.

"That is perfectly obvious!" snapped Robert.

"There had better not be any unexplained appearances of wildlife in Lady Madelyn's bedchamber, my girl, or you will be sorry!" he said sternly to Melanie before he abruptly turned his back to follow Lady Madelyn.

Edward purposefully started to follow him into the dining room, but Lydia put a hand on his arm to detain him.

"Let it go, Edward," she said, looking chagrined. "I am the one at fault here. What I said was unkind and untrue."

"Well, do not let it worry you," Edward said, still indignant on her behalf. "I cannot imagine that Lady Madelyn's outrageous vanity could possibly be injured by anything *we* say. Come along, love, and have some breakfast."

"No," she said, digging in her heels when he would have led her away. A tear coursed down one cheek. "I can't face her. I will just go up to my room."

"I shall have someone bring a tray—"

"No, love," she said, trying without success to smile. "I could not eat a thing."

She hurried out, and Aggie burst into tears of sympathy as Edward followed her.

"Lydia isn't herself now that she's increasing," Robert said, helping Lady Madelyn to all the tastiest morsels from the chafing dishes set out in the dining room.

"Honestly, Robert," Lady Madelyn replied, pointing to a dish of kippers and gesturing for him to put more on her plate when he offered only one, "I wish you would leave off apologizing for something that has nothing to do with you. I am only sorry I gave her the satisfaction of being as catty as she is."

"Even so, there is no excuse for what Lydia said. I should have told her—"

Madelyn smiled affectionately at him. How sweet of Robert to want to be her champion.

"I have heard that particular insult phrased with far more wit than Lydia Whittaker is capable of, and it no longer has the power to hurt me, I promise you," she lied. Actually, she was still fuming, and with the slightest encouragement she could consume the entire serving platter of kippers and all the bacon, too. "The girls at school were quite merciless about my red hair, and they were not satisfied until one of them *did* pull some out by the roots to settle the matter."

"How cruel!" Robert said sympathetically.

"Well," she said with a shrug, "children *are* cruel, you know."

"Not all children," Robert said, looking conscious. "Uh, nothing unusual has happened *here*, has it?"

"Like that mouse in my room, perhaps?"

Robert looked horrified. What a dear man he was!

"Calm yourself, Robert. I was just teasing," she said, smiling. "In case anyone has ambitions in that direction, however, I might just point out I have been subjected to *that* particular trick too often, as well, for it to disturb me overmuch."

Five

Cedric Wyndham returned to the house in high dudgeon after riding about in the everlastingly damp and disagreeable cold looking for Lady Madelyn and that bounder Robert Langtry.

To his additional frustration, he found that Lady Madelyn already had eaten her breakfast and was now ensconced elsewhere in the house, so he had missed his chance, despite his valiant efforts, to press her for an answer to his proposal of marriage.

As he paused inside the drawing-room doorway in the hope that Lady Madelyn might be within, he saw Mrs. Crowley directing some servants in the construction of a little stage near the fireplace. Apparently she was having difficulty in conveying her wishes; at one point she took the hammer from one of the servants and nailed a board into place herself.

Cedric had to admire her competence, even though he suspected that after being compelled to sing silly songs in the freezing cold last night and having been offered no other stimulant than spiced punch to warm himself up with afterward, he would have to endure a performance by a parcel of untalented brats tonight.

He would be forced to smile and pretend to be enjoying himself.

So much for his delightful fantasy of making love

to the rich and exquisite Lady Madelyn during a long, leisurely, *civilized* holiday in a gentleman's country house.

How was he to impress Lady Madelyn with his qualifications as a husband when he couldn't steal two minutes alone with her?

He frowned at one of Mrs. Crowley's tiny daughters when she walked up to him and placed a tentative hand on his knee to get his attention. The little girl's eyes widened at his expression, and she scuttled away, bleating for her mama.

Cedric was appalled that he was capable of scaring off a child with one mean look. And he had the conceit to call himself a diplomat!

"Do not bother Mr. Wyndham, Laura," Mrs. Crowley said, putting one hand to the small of her back and giving him an apologetic smile. Her eyes were tired. Even so, not one dark curl was out of place, and her modest green bombazine gown was free of the creases and dust that one would expect to adhere to the person of someone doing physical labor.

"Yes, Mama," said Laura, looking contrite. He noticed that her identically dressed sister peeped out bashfully from behind her mother's skirt.

Now he *was* ashamed of himself for glaring at the child. They were really quite agreeable little girls, for they weren't given to running around like savages and making an ear-splitting din like the other children here. Cedric had resigned himself with little enthusiasm to the inconvenience of siring some of the noisy, demanding little creatures to propagate his name and hand down his father's title when the time came, but it occurred to him that having children might not be so bad if they were as well-behaved as Mrs. Crowley's daughters. They were rather appealing in their identical blue dresses and their hair in dusky curls.

"Are they twins?" he asked conversationally.

"No," Mrs. Crowley answered, casting a proud eye on her girls. "Laura is thirteen months older and a bit small for her age, while Aimée is a bit big for hers, so I couldn't resist the temptation to dress them alike."

Cedric tried a smile in the chastened little girl's direction and was pleased when Laura's tiny face lit up with pleasure. Emboldened, she scampered right up to him and lifted her arms to be picked up.

"Laura!" cried Mrs. Crowley, scandalized by such forward behavior. "I said you were not to bother Mr. Wyndham!"

The little girl's bottom lip puckered ominously, and Cedric picked her up, gingerly holding her in the crook of his arm. She put her arms around his neck and hugged him.

"Papa," she said.

"Er, no. Sorry," he said, flustered. He felt as if something inside him were melting, which was absurd under the circumstances.

"Laura, dearest," Mrs. Crowley said with a sigh, crossing the room to hold her arms out for her daughter. "Your pardon, Mr. Wyndham. My girls miss their father quite dreadfully, and you *do* resemble him a bit. Of course, Laura knows you are not her father, don't you, Laura?"

"Yes, Mama," the child said wistfully. Before her mother could stop her, Laura placed a butterfly-light kiss on Cedric's smoothly shaved jaw. "Sometimes I like to pretend."

"I know, my dear," she said soothingly as Mr. Wyndham surrendered the little girl to her. She placed her daughter on the floor and gave her a little pat of affection on the top of her head. "Just like you pretend sometimes with Lieutenant Whittaker and Mr. Langtry. But Mr. Wyndham does not know us so well, and we must not impose on his good nature."

"It has not been easy for you," Cedric said sympathetically, and then he felt foolish. It was quite improper of him to make such a personal observation to a virtual stranger.

Fortunately, she took no offense.

"No," she said, smiling bravely. "But one grows accustomed."

She really was not bad looking, Cedric reflected, even though he had been quite put out with her for making him sing those ridiculous songs in the sleigh last night.

Lord! What was he thinking of? The last thing he needed was to be distracted by a pretty widow when a much more advantageous match was within his grasp.

"Have you seen Lady Madelyn?" he asked, forcing his erratic brain to adhere to his object in looking into the drawing room in the first place. "I was hoping I could persuade her to take a walk with me. The winter sunshine is so invigorating."

Lady Madelyn was irrationally fond of snow, and Cedric thought perhaps this would be a way to ingratiate himself with her. Some of his reluctance to renew his acquaintance with the raw weather must have shown in his face, because Mrs. Crowley was surprised into a gurgle of laughter that she hastily turned into a cough.

"If you say so, Mr. Wyndham. For my part, give me a warm corner near the fire and a cup of hot tea on a bitter cold day like this and I am content."

A woman after his own heart, Cedric thought with an inward sigh. If only Lady Madelyn were so sensible.

"I suppose Lady Madelyn is very rich," Mrs. Crowley mused aloud.

"Yes. That is, I believe so," Cedric said, not sure how to reply to this. "What has that to do with anything?"

"Merely that she is spoiled to the bone and only wants what she cannot have, from what Mrs. Whittaker and Mrs. Langtry have told me," Mrs. Crowley said. "If I may venture to give you a hint, Mr. Wyndham, you certainly have made it abundantly obvious that she can have *you* anytime she pleases."

Stung by the unpalatable truth of this, Cedric responded in kind.

"That is a very strange observation coming from someone who persists in pursuing that puffed-up country squire Langtry to the point that a reasonable woman would have given up *that* forlorn hope for lost," he said coolly. "Or has it escaped your notice that he is interested in Lady Madelyn?"

"Of course he is," Mrs. Crowley said, pursing her lips in disapproval. *"Men!* If you are quite at leisure, perhaps you will help us decorate the stage."

"I have better things to do than decorate your blasted stage," he said loftily. Lady Madelyn's indifference to him before these strangers was a sore blow to his pride. "Here is the blasted fellow now."

Cedric scowled when Robert Langtry came into the room with his arms around the shoulders of his nieces, the pretty little blond and the spotty, dark-haired one. Their hostess's younger sisters followed, laughing at something a small fat boy was saying. He was walking backwards in front of them, gesturing exuberantly.

"Mrs. Crowley, how is our production coming

along?'' Mr. Langtry sang out. "These rascals tell me it will be quite a spectacle."

"Indeed, Mr. Langtry." To Cedric's disgust, Mrs. Crowley's peeved expression magically dissolved into a dimpled simper. "And we can certainly use the services of a strong man to help us with the stage."

"I'm at your service," Langtry said, grinning, as he executed a mocking bow. "We saw Lady Madelyn in the hall, and she will join us, too."

Mrs. Crowley's expression hardened.

"How kind of her," she said, sounding less than enthusiastic. She arched one eyebrow at Cedric. "Do you still have better things to do than decorate our blasted stage now that Lady Madelyn is willing to join us?"

"Perhaps I can find the time," he said with a droll look at her to make amends for his churlishness.

By the time Mrs. Crowley and the children had festooned the makeshift stage with boughs of holly and greenery and attached a number of red satin bows to it, the noise level had risen to a barely endurable level despite Mrs. Crowley's admonitions to the children not to disturb the other adults in the house.

Soon they were joined by the boisterous presence of Lord Blakely's twin sons and their doting grandfather, who smiled benevolently as the boys raced about, shrieking with laughter. The Whittaker girls picked up their skirts and chased them, and soon Mrs. Crowley was scowling with impatience because all work had stopped.

To Cedric's horror, a huge, shaggy dog of undetermined parentage lunged into the room and would have jumped up on Cedric's spotless nankeen pantaloons if Cedric's excellent reflexes hadn't come to the rescue. As it was, he stood there, no doubt looking absolutely ridiculous in front of Lady Madelyn, with the dog's forelegs captured in his hands.

Now he wasn't sure what to do with them.

"Look! Mr. Wyndham and Toby are dancing!" shouted the fat little boy. Everyone laughed, and Cedric had no choice but to join in, even though he was seething with frustration.

The boy relieved Cedric of the dog and then, in the apparent misapprehension that he was addressing a fellow dog lover, persisted in prattling at him, so Cedric was slow to fly to the rescue when Lady Madelyn overreached herself trying to place a red bow on the side of the stage and almost toppled off. Langtry was there to catch her, though, and Cedric fumed as he watched the man reverently lift her down from the stage as if she were made of the most delicate porcelain. She smiled up into his eyes, and it took Langtry rather longer than was strictly necessary, in Cedric's opinion, to release her from his grasp.

Cedric racked his brain to come up with a plan to separate them, but Mrs. Crowley's daughters drew him away to see their handiwork on the other side of the stage. Then, before he could come up with a pretext to claim Lady Madelyn's attention, the indecently pregnant Lydia Whittaker waddled through the doorway, wreathed in smiles, as if she would join the group.

She and Lady Madelyn exchanged wary glances. The lieutenant's wife then blushed to the roots of her hair and started to back out of the room.

"Come in," Mrs. Crowley said warmly. "There is plenty of work for all."

"No," the pregnant woman replied, flustered. "Pray excuse me."

She fairly ran from the room.

Lady Madelyn and Langtry exchanged a long look.

"I will go after her," Langtry said.

"No," Lady Madelyn said with a sigh. "It must be me, I'm afraid."

It wasn't hard to run Lydia to ground because her pregnancy made her ungainly. Madelyn took her arm and ushered her right into the parlor.

"Lydia, this is going to be an excessively uncomfortable holiday if you are going to turn red and burst into tears every time you see me," she said with a sigh.

"What I said to you was rude and untrue."

"And I was hardly exercising the highest standard of civility when I stared at your stomach."

"I was jealous because you are always so *perfect* and I feel like a bloated hippopotamus."

"I am hardly perfect. And I was jealous, too."

"Of *me?*" Lydia snorted. "Not likely!"

"Yes. Because you are pregnant."

"You want to be *pregnant?*" Lydia said in astonishment. "What a bouncer!"

"Well, I don't want to be pregnant right *now,*" Madelyn admitted, "but you *did* marry Edward, and I couldn't bring him to scratch even with the lure of a fortune to attract him. I do quite desperately want to have a baby someday before I grow too old."

Lydia stared at her.

"*You* want to have a baby?" Lydia exclaimed.

" 'If you prick us, do we not bleed?' " Madelyn murmured.

"You were jealous of me," Lydia said, apparently finding it hard to believe.

"Well, you don't have to look so pleased about it. Here I am, cast adrift in a positive sea of domestic tranquillity, with no husband and no child. How do you *think* I would feel?"

"You are just trying to make me feel better," Lydia said accusingly.

"Why should I?" asked Madelyn with a shrug.

"You are not still in love with my husband, are you?" Lydia demanded.

Madelyn rolled her eyes. "Certainly not! You may have your precious Edward with my hearty goodwill! Now, dry your eyes and quit turning into a watering pot every time I look at you."

"You could always marry Mr. Wyndham," Lydia suggested.

"Get that gleam out of your eye, Lydia Whittaker!" Madelyn snapped. "There is quite enough match-making going on at this party, thank you very much! Now, let us join the others before we have the good lieutenant in here threatening to call me out."

Lydia gave a gurgle of laughter.

"Darling Edward is *so* overprotective."

"There! You see? You are doing it on purpose," Madelyn said in a mock-injured tone.

Lydia gave her a thoughtful look.

"Lady Letitia says you and Mr. Wyndham are perfect for one another."

"Perhaps," Madelyn said thoughtfully. "I, too, was half-convinced we might suit before—but that is neither here nor there."

"Before you saw Robert again, I suppose," Lydia said. "Does he know you are still in love with him?"

"Lydia Whittaker! If you *dare* make such a ridiculous suggestion to him, I shall *strangle* you, baby or no baby!"

"Pamela Crowley is perfect for him," Lydia said with a sigh. "His mother even likes her."

"I, on the other hand, am a selfish spinster who

would callously send his poor brother's children to boarding school and abandon Robert for my frivolous life of dissipation on the Continent," Madelyn said bitterly. She gave a snort of cynical laughter when Lydia stared at her in dismay. "Do you think I don't know what all of you are saying behind my back?"

Lydia hung her head.

"All I want is for Robert to be happy," Lydia said. "It isn't easy for a bachelor to rear four children alone, for his mother certainly has been little help."

"And if he marries Mrs. Crowley," Madelyn said shrewdly, "his mother needn't worry that he is going to leave the children on her hands while he goes off to start his own household with his bride. If, on the other hand, he marries a lady with property of her own, he will no longer be tied to Mrs. Langtry's apron strings. I am well aware that the property is hers until after her death, and Robert is merely her heir. My guardian looked carefully into his prospects when he asked for permission to pay his addresses to me, I promise you."

"Mrs. Langtry is only thinking of Robert's happiness!"

"Of course," Madelyn said, seeing that Lydia was becoming agitated again. "At any rate, we are just friends now. There is a vast difference between wanting an infant to cuddle in my arms and marrying the guardian of four great, grown creatures like the Langtry children."

"You would tire of him in a twelvemonth," Lydia said.

"Can you see *me* buried in Yorkshire and doing good works?" Madelyn said, forcing herself to smile.

"No," Lydia said, smiling back. She looked relieved, as if the question had been settled. "Mrs. Crowley would be much better for him."

"If you say so," Madelyn said skeptically. "I personally don't think he is that attracted to her, and I don't think my presence has anything to do with it."

"I am afraid you're right. Gentlemen are *so* provoking! They always seem to want what isn't good for them."

And, Madelyn supposed, Lydia thought that Robert wanted *her.*

Well, she was wrong. He had chosen once between Madelyn and his wards, and he would make the same choice again if she was foolish enough to reveal her love for him.

Lieutenant Whittaker stalked into the room and narrowed his eyes at the sight of his wife on the sofa with tears drying on her blotched face and Madelyn sitting beside her.

"What did you say to her, Lady Madelyn?" he asked. His voice was soft and controlled, but Madelyn could hear the steel behind it.

"Oh, for pity's sake, I didn't say a *word* to your precious wife!" Madelyn snapped, and left the parlor so they could bill and coo to their heart's content. She heard Lydia call out after her, but she kept walking and went straight to her room with every intention of pleading a headache and staying there until dinner.

She didn't feel like proper company for anyone at the moment.

But Madelyn wasn't destined to find peace.

She heard a scurry of footsteps and a whisper as soon as she entered her room and found *two* of them on her bed this time.

". . . and she must have brought twenty pairs of shoes!" Mary was saying to Matthew. The boy was holding Madelyn's silver-handled brush almost reverently. They both looked up guiltily when Madelyn appeared.

It seemed Mary was not the only one who missed her late mother—or rather, her late mother's sybaritic taste—and her heart went out to the plainly uncomfortable little boy. He obviously was embarrassed to be caught disporting himself among a lady's clothing.

"Lady Madelyn!" Mary said, looking at Madelyn with every evidence of pleasure. "Matthew came with me today. I hope you do not mind."

"No, not at all," Madelyn said, and realized it was true.

"Are you going to tell Uncle Robert we were here?" Matthew asked with a heartbreakingly anxious look on his face.

"I don't believe it is any of his business whom I entertain in my suite," Madelyn said with a bit of hauteur in her tone. "I find I am perishing for a cup of tea all of a sudden."

"And some of the macaroons Lady Blakely's cook makes?" Matthew said, brightening.

"Precisely! Since Bettina has gone to visit her family, perhaps you will wait here while I arrange for some. You must be very quiet, though, or we shall be found out."

Madelyn retraced her steps to the floor below with a little smile on her lips. It was nice to be appreciated for a change.

"What is the meaning of this!" cried Mrs. Crowley when she burst into Madelyn's suite with Robert at her heels.

Matthew was caught with a macaroon in his mouth and started to choke. His sister's efforts to pound him on the back upset Madelyn's teacup and sent a shower of tepid liquid to soak into the yellow muslin of her gown.

Madelyn regarded Mrs. Crowley's outraged countenance with a wry grimace.

"Is it not obvious?" she scoffed. "I lured the children into my room and plied them with macaroons so that when I've fattened them up sufficiently, I may roast them in the oven with carrots and potatoes and *eat* them."

Robert, who had looked aghast when the tea spilled, gave a hastily stifled bark of laughter.

"Are you all right, Matthew?" he asked, going to the boy's other side.

"Look at the mess you've made!" Mrs. Crowley scolded the boy. "And having refreshments with dinner a mere two hours away!"

"I was hungry," Madelyn said, daring her to say more.

The dreadful woman huffed a little but was silenced.

"If there is nothing else?" Madelyn said politely, eyebrows raised.

Mrs. Crowley departed in a huff, but the children wiped the grins off their faces at a pained look from Robert.

"Lady Madelyn, if the children are disturbing you—"

"Mary and Matthew are here as my *invited* guests, Mr. Langtry," Madelyn said pointedly. Never mind that she was stretching the truth a bit.

"I see." He bowed stiffly. "In that case, I will apologize for the intrusion and take myself off."

"Stay, Uncle Robert!" Matthew said, holding out one chubby hand endearingly encrusted with macaroon crumbs. Mary scooted over to make room for him at the tiny tea table. "We never get bang-up refreshments like this in the nursery! Look, there's a cake, too. And these little custard things with chocolate on them."

"Eclairs," Mary said, sounding superior.

"Well, it would hardly be proper for me to—" Robert began, looking regretful.

"*Do* stop being such a fusty old stick, Mr. Langtry," Madelyn said with a wave of her hand toward the space that Mary and Matthew had made for him. "I agree it is not *quite* the thing for you to have refreshments in a lady's room, but I venture to say we are more than adequately chaperoned."

Six

Christmas pageants are for babies.

Melanie stoically stood her ground on the stage behind the smaller children and tried to remember the words of the stupid song she was supposed to sing.

Her younger sister, Mary, looked adorable with her hair tied up in pretty curls and shiny gold ribbon. She had emerged from Lady Madelyn's room, proud as a peacock, in this guise. She was supposed to be an angel, and she certainly looked the part. So did Laura and Aimée in their little halos of golden tinsel.

Melanie, on the other hand, had her hair slicked straight back, so the horrid spots on her forehead and her fat cheeks fairly shouted to be noticed.

She was a shepherd.

Not that it mattered.

Who *cared* about a stupid Christmas pageant, anyway.

All the adults were gathered in chairs in front of the stage, and Uncle Robert sent a smile her way, probably hoping she would smile back at him.

Well, she did, of course, but that didn't mean she was going to *enjoy* standing up there making a fool of herself. Mary was preening and waving to Lady Madelyn, who gave her a flirtatious wiggle of her fingers back.

Mary would be insufferable for the rest of the evening, Melanie thought resentfully. Naturally, Lady Madelyn and all the other ladies liked Mary best. Even when she said something stupid, it sounded cute. Mary was forever sneaking off to Lady Madelyn's room so that she could come back all superior with stories about Lady Madelyn's travels. Lady Madelyn even gave her things, like bits of ribbons and artificial flowers.

Lady Madelyn reminded Mary of Mama. She said she even wore perfume from Paris like Mama, and when Melanie was skeptical, she invited Melanie to go along to Lady Madelyn's room for a sniff of her clothes.

Melanie wasn't about to do so. *She* would probably be sent about her business. She knew perfectly well that Lady Madelyn didn't like *her.*

Aggie and Amy Whittaker were seated at the pianoforte, where they were to accompany the singers. They were dressed in pretty dresses, Melanie thought enviously, instead of in a man's old dressing gown with a ratty old sash, which didn't look like a shepherd's costume in the least!

Melanie regretted that she had refused to practice when Uncle Robert arranged for Mrs. Crowley to give her and Mary music instructions. Mrs. Crowley didn't like her, either, and was forever scolding her for not doing as well as Mary at her lessons.

Mary, of course, practiced all the time and often entertained Uncle Robert's guests. He was disappointed because Melanie refused to show off for a parcel of cooing, cheek-pinching strangers as well!

This time Mrs. Crowley had left her no choice, and Uncle Robert had backed her up. He was forever telling her she had a wonderful voice and that it would be a pity if Lord Blakely's guests were deprived of hearing it.

Too bad they had to *look* at her at the same time, Melanie thought bitterly.

When Mrs. Crowley gave the signal to start, Melanie obediently opened her mouth and started to sing. It was a nice song, really, although she hadn't heard it before Mrs. Crowley taught it to them that afternoon.

Melanie was supposed to deepen her voice like a man's, but she soon forgot and was singing in her natural voice. She realized she was drowning out the younger children when Mary turned around to look at her once and Mrs. Crowley directed a frown in her direction.

Mortified, she started singing more softly. All her pleasure in the song was ended because she had made a fool of herself.

Again.

That's when she saw Lady Madelyn lean over and touch Uncle Robert's arm. He inclined his head politely when she whispered something to him, and he nodded. They both seemed to be looking straight at *her.*

When the song was over, she and Mary were to leave the stage because Laura and Aimée were going to sing a duet. When she got to the bottom step, she saw that Lady Madelyn was waiting for them. Melanie turned away, assuming she was there to talk to Mary, but Lady Madelyn put a hand on Melanie's shoulder as well and guided both of the girls out into the hallway.

"I knew some repairs would be needed," Lady Madelyn whispered as she withdrew some hairpins from her reticule and anchored some of Mary's curls more firmly. "And Melanie, I hope you will indulge me. I have been perishing to get my hands on your hair."

How humiliating.

Lady Madelyn felt *sorry* for her, so she was going to try to do something with her hair.

"It's supposed to look this way," Melanie said, embarrassed. "I'm a shepherd."

"I understand that," Lady Madelyn said as she deftly removed the horrid robe to reveal Melanie's yellow dress, "but I am quite sure no actress on the London stage would let mere conformity to a role keep her from looking her best. If you will permit me?"

Melanie really didn't have any choice. Lady Madelyn was already undoing the ribbon that held her hair in a stubby queue at the nape of her neck.

"What wonderful hair," Lady Madelyn said admiringly. "So thick and shiny. Mary, hold these pins for me, if you please."

Mary, of course, looked as if an angel had come down from heaven and spoken to her.

"What we need is a pair of nice, thick, shiny braids to twist around your head like a crown."

"It looks wonderful already," Melanie heard Uncle Robert say. *He must be looking over Lady Madelyn's shoulder.* Melanie had not seen him come out of the room, and she flinched.

Lady Madelyn gave a persecuted sigh.

"There, you startled her, and now I have to start over," she said. "Go away, Mr. Langtry."

He did not obey; like Mary, he was too busy fawning over her.

"You missed some," he pointed out, touching a stray strand of Melanie's hair that escaped to tease the side of her face.

"I did it deliberately," Madelyn said. "It looks

softer this way. She has lovely eyes, and this shows them off to advantage."

Melanie felt her eyes grow moist. This close to Lady Madelyn she could tell she *did* smell like Mama. Mama had always insisted that a lady wasn't ready to meet the day until she had anointed her body with some delicious scent. Melanie remembered how her mother used to comb her hair until it shone like glass.

And when she did, her beautiful perfume would envelop Melanie and make her think of exotic flowers and magic carpets.

"Very pretty," Robert said, his voice sounding a bit quivery. "You look so much like your mother with your hair like that, Melanie. I never saw it before."

Melanie's mother was blond, like Mary and Matthew, and Melanie had always thought she was the most beautiful lady in the world. Uncle Robert was just trying to be nice. Even so, Melanie stood a bit straighter. With her hair up, she felt like a swan.

"Now, Mary, I'm afraid I have to ask you to part with some of your ribbons," Lady Madelyn said. "Oh, my dear, did I hurt you?" she added when Melanie flinched.

"I don't mind," Melanie said softly, even though the hairpin jabbed her scalp.

"You know, Melanie would sing quite marvelously well if she had the benefit of good instruction," Lady Madelyn was saying to Uncle Robert. "I should like for my old singing master to hear her, if you have no objection. He was living in London the last time we corresponded. I shall send a letter to his last address to see what can be arranged."

Melanie's one vanity and Lady Madelyn had put her finger square upon it.

"Do you really think so?" Uncle Robert said,

sounding pleased. "I have always thought her voice quite extraordinary myself, but I might be pardoned for being prejudiced."

"No, you aren't prejudiced," Lady Madelyn said coolly. "She *is* extraordinary, or she will be when she applies herself."

Melanie's eyes narrowed.

Lady Madelyn was a devious one, all right. Melanie didn't believe for a minute that a great lady like her would put herself out to gratify her.

She's after Uncle Robert, of course, Melanie thought bitterly, and she almost fell for her cozening ways.

Well, Lady Madelyn had already won over Mary and Matthew, and Mark—being almost a man—was inclined to admire her as well. But Melanie was not so easy to fool.

"I can take her to London at his convenience anytime he has leisure to see her," Uncle Robert said. "We can stay with Eleanor's parents. They would love to see the children."

"I don't want to go to London," Melanie said, gritting her teeth. "You're only being nice to us because you want to marry Uncle Robert."

Nearly blinded by tears, she quickly moved away from the perfumed cloud of sweet insincerity that was Lady Madelyn and went to stand by Amy and Aggie by the pianoforte.

"Your hair is so pretty," Aggie said, reaching up with a gentle finger to touch the strand at Melanie's cheek. "Let us go into the other room so you can see it in the mirror."

"Yes," Melanie said, grateful for the chance to escape from the room. She had been rude to Lady Madelyn, and Uncle Robert was giving her that sad, reproachful look he had sometimes. "But don't you have to play?"

"Amy can play until I get back, can't you, Amy?"

"Of course," the other girl said, keeping an eye on Mrs. Crowley for the signal to begin the next song. "But be sure to return before they sing 'The Twelve Days of Christmas,' because I don't know that one."

As it turned out, the company was not destined to hear "The Twelve Days of Christmas" at all that night because just as Matthew and James and Jeremy finished doing a little jig on the stage, Lydia Whittaker gave a great cry of mingled pain and surprise, then doubled over.

"Lydia!" exclaimed her husband, putting his arms around her. "Darling, it isn't the baby, is it?"

"I'm afraid so," she said ruefully. "He has been making his presence known for quite some time, but I didn't want to disturb anyone."

"Didn't want to disturb anyone!" Edward said, close to panic. "Blakely! Send for the doctor!"

Alexander raced from the room as Lydia's mother, her sisters, Mrs. Crowley, and Mrs. Langtry converged upon Lydia and her husband in a determined circle.

The younger children, frightened by the expressions of alarm on the adults' faces, started whimpering and crying.

"Calm yourselves. This baby will come in his own sweet time," Lydia said. Then she gave a little laugh of surprise and embarrassment as her husband gallantly scooped her up in his arms and carried her toward the doorway.

"Edward, you silly man!" she scolded lovingly. "There is no need to make such a piece of work of it! I can walk perfectly well on my own two legs!"

"Humor me, my love," he said in a choked voice. "If anything goes wrong with you or our child, I will never forgive myself."

"You would think no one ever had a baby before," Lydia said, but Madelyn could tell she was pleased by her husband's solicitude.

Well, why shouldn't she be?

It was obvious that her husband loved her very much.

Robert had a hand on Aggie's and Amy's shoulders, preventing them from their obvious intention of joining the company of matriarchs escorting the lieutenant and their elder sister to her bedroom.

Madelyn felt a tentative tug on her skirts and looked down to see that Mary had come to her side. Her little brow was puckered with worry. Madelyn bent down to put an arm around the little girl's shoulders.

"Me, too," said Matthew softly as he moved around to Madelyn's other side so she could hug him as well.

Madelyn was absurdly touched that they sought her out for comfort. She guided the children to a sofa and spoke soothingly to them as the others milled around, looking uncertain. She was surprised to see that both Laura and Aimée sought comfort on Mr. Wyndham's lap, and he was patting them both awkwardly.

"Ah, there you are," Robert said, stepping in front of Madelyn. "Come along, children. It is time for you to go to bed."

Madelyn expected them to object. How could he expect them to go tamely to bed with all the excitement in the house? But they rose to take the hands he reached out to them.

Robert smiled gratefully at Madelyn.

"Thank you for taking care of them, Lady Madelyn," he said warmly. "You're very kind."

"It was my pleasure," Madelyn said solemnly.

The next morning, Madelyn could see that Vanessa was trying hard to be a gracious hostess, but her heart wasn't in it. Her sister was lying in her bedroom with the doctor and her husband in anxious attendance, and her mother was in a terrible state. Mrs. Whittaker, a lady of exquisite sensibility, reacted to any crisis, it seemed, with a fit of the vapors.

Mrs. Crowley proved her mettle by appropriating some of the responsibilities of hostess with the result that she was considered indispensable both in the lying-in room and the rest of the household. Vanessa was almost incoherently grateful. Pamela Crowley's domestic skills, Madelyn admitted grudgingly, had not been exaggerated in the least.

Even so, there were rather too many people in the house, and Madelyn was determined not to add to Lady Blakely's burdens.

"I believe it would be best if I left," she told a hollow-eyed Vanessa while Lydia remained upstairs sleeping fitfully between labor pains. The future mother had been right; the baby would come in its own sweet time. Those who slept in the west wing were kept awake by the lady's groans and the running feet of various family members and servants desperate to give her relief.

"Please don't feel you have to leave because of the baby," Vanessa said, sacrificing truth on the altar of good manners. "You know we would be delighted to have you stay as long as you wish."

"Of course, my dear," Madelyn said, giving Vanessa's hand a reassuring pat. "You and Alexander have been all that is hospitable, and I have had a delightful stay so far. But this is a special time for you and your family, and I do not wish to intrude where I cannot possibly be of assistance."

Vanessa gave her a wry smile.

"Well, I am persuaded you were not presented with entertainment like this in all your years on the Continent."

Madelyn had to laugh.

"No, indeed! A baby nearly dropped in the middle of the drawing room certainly is a novelty."

"I must say this is quite unlike Lydia," Vanessa said with a glimmer of humor. "She was persuaded she would not have the baby until she was safely home in Yorkshire, and it never occurred to any of us that she might be wrong. As a rule, she is so dependable."

"She is in no danger, is she?" Madelyn asked in concern. "Because the baby is coming earlier than expected?"

"The doctor says not," Vanessa said, looking worried, "but all of us are excessively anxious, as you must know."

Robert walked into the room at this moment and looked surprised to see the two women together, as well he might. They had not been especially friendly in the past, which was not remarkable considering that Lady Letitia and the earl had been determined to persuade Alexander to marry Madelyn instead of the insignificant Vanessa Whittaker and had almost been barred from Alexander and Vanessa's wedding because of it.

"Robert! Do sit down and have a cup of tea," Vanessa said, mindful of her responsibilities as hostess.

"Thank you, Vanessa," he said, "but I haven't the

time. I just wanted to tell you that the children and I have decided to go home early."

Vanessa stifled her expression of relief with difficulty.

"Are you sure, Robert? The children—"

"My dear, I hope you are not going to stand on ceremony with *me!* You are wishing all of your guests to the devil, I can imagine." He made a gallant bow in Madelyn's direction. "Present charming company excepted, of course."

"You and Lady Madelyn must be the most considerate persons on earth," Vanessa said in relief.

Robert gave Madelyn a questioning look.

"I am leaving as well, Mr. Langtry," she said with a tight smile.

"You must take Alice along for propriety's sake," Vanessa said politely. "I insist!"

Alice was the house servant who had been assigned to Madelyn when it became apparent that Lady Letitia's dresser would not have the time to serve two so demandingly fashionable ladies and Madelyn's attempts to keep her own things in order had resulted in a hopeless muddle.

Madelyn was uncomfortably aware that her decision to send her maid on a family visit had made it necessary for Vanessa to spare a servant for Madelyn's use from a household staff that was already spread too thin with so many guests in the house.

Vanessa must be very glad to see the back of her, Madelyn thought wryly, if she was willing to spare Alice for her journey.

"You are very kind. I will send her back on the stagecoach," Madelyn promised.

"It is the least we can do. I am so sorry to upset your plans for the holiday," Vanessa said, which

Madelyn thought extremely courteous, since she had not invited Madelyn to come in the first place.

"Nonsense! I had planned to go on alone to Yorkshire, anyway, to see in the New Year with my cousins, for I knew Lord Stoneham and Lady Letitia would want to go back in the direction of London rather than north when they left here. The only difference is that I will be leaving a bit sooner than I had planned."

"I wish you would agree to travel with us," Robert said, "since we are going in the same direction. It would be our pleasure."

"Hardly," Madelyn said, giving him a skeptical smile.

"I must own, I would be easier in my mind if you would agree to travel with Robert and his mother," Vanessa ventured. "A woman alone—"

"—in her own coach with a coachman, her own extremely brawny guard, and Vanessa's Alice to watch over her," Madelyn pointed out with a glimmer of humor. "I will be only a few days on the road, after all."

"We will be going by easy stages, of course, because of the children, so it would take you longer to reach your destination if you go with us," Robert persisted, "but—"

"*No*, Robert," Madelyn interrupted. "We have already had this discussion, if you will recall! But I thank you for your concern."

"If you are quite certain, there is no more to say. Lady Madelyn, Robert," Vanessa said, rising. "If you will excuse me, I should like to visit Lydia and see if there is anything she requires."

"Of course," Madelyn said, rising also.

Robert stood and allowed the ladies to precede him from the room, but Madelyn could see that his lips were tightly clamped shut, as if to prevent an unwise utterance from escaping. As soon as Vanessa parted company from them in order to proceed to her sister's place of confinement, Robert renewed his objections.

"Madelyn, upon reflection I cannot like this idea of your traveling to Yorkshire alone," he said. "Something might happen to you."

"Nothing so very bad is going to happen to me if I go to Yorkshire alone, Robert," Madelyn said sadly. "Not to compare with what might happen to me if I go with you. Can you see *me* traveling with four children and your mother? You will not be doing them or me any favors, I promise you."

Robert bowed his head in defeat.

"You are right, of course," he said, and left her.

It would not have worked out, Madelyn thought, regretting that she could not have had more time with him. Staying with him here, seeing him every day, had been a delicious sort of torture.

She would never again, as long as she lived, love any man as much as she loved Robert Langtry.

It was impossible. Absolutely impossible.

Madelyn had many talents, none of which were of the slightest use to the bachelor guardian of four children.

She didn't know how children thought. She didn't know what they wanted. She certainly didn't know what they needed.

Truth to tell, they terrified her almost as much as this undying passion she had for Robert Langtry.

If she spent days in close confinement with him and them on this journey, he would see her for the inadequate, empty person she had become.

Madelyn could shine in a ballroom or a drawing room, but take her out of her Paris gowns and her artificial environment and she was as awkward as a duck out of water.

Better that they should part now, when he could still have some respect for her.

"The baby! The baby!"

Mary was almost incoherent with glee as she ran into Madelyn's room, where she was directing Alice in the packing of her gowns.

The joy faded from the child's face.

"What are you doing?" she asked, looking shocked. "You're not leaving! *Please* don't go!"

"I must, I'm afraid," Madelyn said, feeling like a villain because Mary looked so dismayed. She told herself that Mary would not miss her as much as she would miss her gowns and her hats.

"This is all Melanie's fault, and so I shall tell her!" Mary said, looking angry.

"What is this about a baby?" Madelyn said, thinking a distraction was in order.

"It's a boy," said Mary, but her earlier pleasure obviously was quite ruined. "They are going to name him Quentin Alexander."

"A very fine name, to be sure," Madelyn said. "Have you seen him yet?"

"No. Mrs. Crowley is going to bring him into the drawing room so we can all see him. Will you not come with me?"

"I should be delighted," Madelyn said, summoning a smile to her lips. "How pleased Lieutenant Whittaker must be!"

"Let us go at once," Mary said, putting her hand trustfully in Madelyn's. "Mrs. Crowley says she will not let him out of the bedroom for long, for it would be a terrible thing if he were to catch cold."

Along the way, they encountered Matthew, who took Madelyn's free hand and prattled happily to her as they walked through the nursery wing.

They entered the drawing room to find Mrs. Crowley and Robert cooing over Master Quentin Alexander Whittaker, who was sleeping obliviously through all the racket being made by a roomful of excited children and tearful adults.

"My grandson," Mrs. Whittaker said, weeping softly as Mrs. Langtry patted her on the shoulder. "He has such a look of George, don't you think? Such a handsome little fellow."

Madelyn had not known Mrs. Whittaker's late husband, so she was no judge, but she didn't think the child looked like anybody or any*thing* in her experience. She had never seen a newborn before, and she was quite shocked by how painfully raw and tender its skin looked. Its face seemed all pushed in beneath a delicate tracery of wispy hair.

Then baby Quentin opened his eyes and looked right at Madelyn, even though his gaze seemed unfocused. He opened his tiny mouth and displayed pink, toothless gums in what Madelyn could have sworn was a smile.

Simple as that, Madelyn was in love.

"Oooooh," she breathed through the sentimental tears that sprang to her eyes and the lump that formed in her throat. "He's so beautiful."

Mrs. Crowley looked at her with something that was almost approval.

"No matter how many children you have, each one is a miracle," she whispered in a wistful voice. "Would you like to hold him? I think my girls will need some reassurance that I still love them best."

"Oh, I *couldn't*," Madelyn blurted out, panicked. "He's so small, I might—"

"Break him?" Mrs. Crowley said with a superior laugh, although there was a good deal of kindness in it. "Not likely! Sit down on the sofa and hold out your arms. I'll hand him to you. Just be sure to support his neck."

With that, she placed the soft, warm little scrap of humanity into Madelyn's arms, and Madelyn's heart turned over. She couldn't resist touching the tiny, perfect hand, and she gave a little moan of pleasure when the small fingers curled around hers. They were as pale and graceful as the tentacles of a sea anemone.

"A fine fellow, aren't you?" Robert said in her ear as he put his arm around her and leaned over her shoulder to get a better look at the child.

Matthew and Mary crowded in on either side. Mary managed to climb into Robert's lap and touch the baby's cheek. Mark stood behind the sofa and loomed over Madelyn and the child so he could see the baby's face.

Melanie was standing so close behind Madelyn that she felt the girl's breath on her hair.

"Me next!" begged Melanie. When Madelyn looked up at her, she saw that the surly look was gone from Melanie's face and was replaced by something akin to radiance. "Oh, *please* can I hold him?"

"Maybe tomorrow," the ever-vigilant Mrs. Crowley called out from where she was enthroned in a chair, cuddling and talking softly to Laura and Aimée. Then she brought both her daughters to admire the baby. "It is time for me to take this young man back to his mother."

To a chorus of universal protests, Mrs. Crowley retrieved the baby and carried him away after making sure every bit of young Quentin Alexander was covered, even his face, by a soft blanket.

"Dear Pamela is so good with children," Mrs. Langtry said complacently. She gave her son a pointed look. "She would make some lucky man such a good wife!"

Nothing subtle about that!

But Mrs. Langtry no longer needed to worry that Madelyn was going to set a snare for her precious son.

No one knew better than Madelyn that Robert would be a fool to marry Madelyn instead of some paragon of motherly and wifely virtue like Pamela Crowley.

Being accepted for a short while in the loving Whittaker family circle had done something quite serious to Madelyn's heart, and she knew she would never feel quite so smug in her own superiority again.

Seven

Dinner that night was even more boisterous than usual.

The birth of a child into such a loving family apparently was something to be celebrated, even though the ecstatic new parents themselves were dining privately in Lydia's bedroom.

Instead of conversing in decorous tones to the persons on the right and left at proper intervals, the happy diners called out comments and joking remarks across the table. There were plenty of youthful high spirits in the company tonight.

Although on all previous evenings the twins, Mary, Matthew, Laura, and Aimée were fed by the nursery staff some hours before the adults enjoyed their formal meal, as a special treat they were permitted to dine with the adults. Miss Mary Ann Whittaker, their hostess's younger sister, had just arrived from London, which was another cause for celebration.

Unfortunately, this festive atmosphere lulled Robert's eldest ward into thinking that the rules were as flexible here as they were at home in the country.

Cedric Wyndham looked shocked when Mark left his place at table and reached over the older man to snatch both turkey legs from the platter in front of him.

"Mark!" cried Robert, shocked by this lapse in his

ward's manners. "Sit down at once and wait for the food to be passed to you."

"Yes, Uncle Robert," the youth said meekly, reddening about the ears.

At home they were in the habit of letting Mark have the legs of whatever fowl they were eating because he liked them so much and none of the other children particularly wanted them.

Of course, darting about the table snatching one's favorite bits from beneath the very noses of the other guests was simply not done in company, and Mark certainly should have known better.

If he didn't, Robert had no one to blame but himself.

Robert had been lax in insisting on proper decorum at the dinner table, at first because he could not bear to reprimand his grieving wards for any reason and then out of sheer sloth. It was simply easier to let them do what they wished instead of insisting on better behavior. Robert began to think that perhaps his mother and Mrs. Crowley were right and he did the children no great favor by being so easygoing when it came to discipline.

Mr. Wyndham, Lady Letitia, and the earl looked utterly appalled. Lady Madelyn and Mrs. Crowley tactfully pretended to be deaf and blind to the incident, and their hostess merely smiled reassuringly at Mark as he slouched uncomfortably in his seat. Melanie had started to reach in front of Aggie for a piece of bread but wisely withdrew her hand before she could share in her brother's disgrace.

"The snow has finally stopped, thank heaven," Vanessa said to distract everyone's attention from the disgraced youth. "Are you still determined to leave in the morning, Madelyn? Perhaps you should wait another day to be sure the roads are cleared."

"Thank you, no," Madelyn said with a smile. "I am anxious to see my cousin again, and my guardian, Mr. Kenniston. His widowed sister and my cousin Elizabeth share a charming house on his estate in Yorkshire. Elizabeth, if you will recall, was my companion for years after I left school. She is enjoying a well-earned retirement now from trying to keep me in order. Mr. Kenniston will meet us there."

"I remember your cousin quite well, of course. I hope she and Mr. Kenniston enjoy good health."

"So do I," Madelyn said, looking a little worried. "I fear that I have not paid proper attention to the few relatives I have left."

Robert realized at that moment just how much Madelyn had changed from the girl he knew years ago. The old Madelyn had nothing but resentment for the middle-aged caretakers who were determined to spoil all her pleasure by insisting that she conduct herself with the decorum expected of an earl's daughter. Madelyn often had referred to Elizabeth unkindly as her watchdog and accused her of spying on her so she could bear tales to Mr. Kenniston. Now, it seemed, she had some fondness for them, after all.

It was just more evidence of how she had matured.

The old Madelyn, for instance, would not have been so tolerant of children at the dinner table, he thought as he saw Madelyn pass a dish of buttered lobsters to Aggie, who wrinkled her nose and smilingly shook her head.

Melanie regarded Madelyn with surly indifference when she caught the girl staring at her and proffered the dish.

Robert sighed.

Tomorrow he and Madelyn would both be gone from here, and he most probably would not see her again. All he had to do was restrain himself from acting like a lovesick fool until then.

Mr. Wyndham, Robert thought with pardonable satisfaction, would be put out by her departure. He either would have to stay as long as Lady Letitia and Lord Stoneham, since he had come at their invitation, or make his own way elsewhere by hired chaise or by stagecoach. The poor devil had hoped, no doubt, to escort Lady Madelyn to Yorkshire for an introduction to her guardian as a prospective betrothed husband.

Robert could almost pity him.

Almost.

If Robert could not have Madelyn, it gave him some small comfort to know that Mr. Wyndham could not have her, either.

At least not yet.

Madelyn looked across the table at Robert with an expression of inquiry on her face, for all the world as if he had spoken out loud. Perhaps she could sense his gaze upon her.

Robert just stared back, memorizing the lovely picture she made in yet another of her sumptuous evening gowns. This one was made of emerald-green satin and was a perfect foil for her dramatic coloring. Her beautiful face was framed by a loosely confined riot of careless curls set with emerald clips. It looked as if the whole fiery mass would come down in a sensuous fall at a man's touch. Matching emeralds graced her slender neck and earlobes.

She looked away, obviously put out of countenance by his scrutiny.

What business had a clod like him to covet such loveliness, he thought with vicious self-loathing.

"You are not hungry tonight, Mr. Langtry?" asked

Pamela Crowley innocently. "May I tempt you with some of this excellent herring?"

He found himself seated next to her at almost every meal, thanks to the less-than-subtle matchmakers in residence. Fortunately, she seemed to have given up her pursuit of him as a prospective husband and he could be easy in her company.

"Yes, I thank you, Mrs. Crowley," he said, forcing himself to turn his gaze away from Madelyn.

His companion held the serving dish so he could spoon some of the fish onto his plate.

He did so reluctantly, for he had accepted her offer merely as a diversion.

Robert *hated* pickled herring! It served him right to have to swallow the reeking stuff, he thought as he smiled at Mrs. Crowley and took his punishment like a man.

Later, despite his best intentions, the sight of Madelyn standing pensively under one of Vanessa's infernal kissing boughs was too much temptation when he surprised her in the entryway on his way to the upper floor. The younger children should have been in bed, but Robert knew Mary and Matthew would not go to sleep until he visited them in the nursery to read them a story. To that end, Robert had excused himself from the dining room, where the gentlemen were lingering over their port. He had assumed Madelyn and all the other ladies were still in the parlor diverting themselves with refreshments and gossip.

Madelyn gave a gasp of surprise when Robert took her in his arms and captured her lips with his. She resisted for a moment, and then she gave a little sigh of surrender and kissed him back.

Before he could follow up on this invitation to further explore her beautiful mouth, the big, shaggy dog that was the twins' near-constant companion burst into the entryway pursued by a barefooted Matthew in his nightshirt. After him ran Melanie, who stopped, stricken, at the sight of Lady Madelyn in Robert's embrace.

"Lady Madelyn! Look!" came a childish voice from high above them. "Aggie said I could keep her kitten with me tonight!"

Madelyn gave a strangled cry, and Robert turned to follow the direction of her horrified gaze. Mary was leaning precariously over the railing and probably would have tumbled over the side if Mark had not grabbed her by the back of her night rail. As it was, the startled child dropped the small charcoal-colored kitten she had been holding in her hands, and it was falling toward the floor.

"Save him, Uncle Robert!" Mary cried.

As Robert stepped into the airborne kitten's path and braced himself with hunched shoulders, Madelyn squeezed her eyes shut in anticipation of the impact.

The kitten landed with a terrified yowl on Robert's back and dug its needle-sharp claws into his best coat of dark blue superfine. It tore the fabric a fraction of an inch and then stuck there.

Mark and Mary, by this time, had rushed down the steps. Mark detached the kitten from the back of Robert's coat and got his fingers scratched for his pains.

"You saved him, Uncle Robert," Mary said, radiantly grateful.

"What are you doing out of bed, Mary?" Robert demanded. His heart was still hammering in his chest, because it could have been his precious niece, and not the kitten, to tumble over the railing toward the cold marble floor below.

Mary hung her head at his brusque tone.

Robert was instantly ashamed of himself. He got down on one knee so he would be at her level and touched her cheek.

"Love, you could have been hurt," he said, trying to make her understand why he had sounded so angry. "If something happened to you—" He broke off because he couldn't finish the thought without disgracing himself yet again in front of Madelyn. Unmanly displays of emotion were *not* acceptable in polite company.

Mary threw both of her thin arms around his neck. "I'm sorry, Uncle Robert," she said.

"You're a good girl, Mary," Robert said, hugging her. "Now, go on up to bed. I will join you in a moment."

He turned his attention to Matthew, who looked as if he knew he was in disgrace, and gave him a wry smile.

"Come along, Matt," he said, holding out his arms.

Matthew ran into them with an expression of joyful relief on his face and hugged his uncle the way his sister had.

"Off to bed, and take the dog with you, if you please," Robert said. The little girl accepted the kitten that Mark restored to her and walked over to Madelyn with the obvious intention of showing it off to her. Madelyn merely shook her head at her. It was curious behavior, but Robert thought perhaps Madelyn, too, had been shaken by the tragedy that had been so narrowly averted and was too overcome to speak. "Mary? Matthew? To bed. *Now*, if you please."

"Yes, Uncle Robert," Mary and Matthew chorused. Mary turned obediently to climb the stairs, but Mat-

We'd Like to Invite You to Subscribe to Zebra's Regency Romance Book Club and Give You a Gift of 4 Free Books as Your Introduction! (Worth $19.96!)

If you're a Regency lover, imagine the joy of getting **4 FREE Zebra Regency Romances** and then the chance to have these lovely stories delivered to your home each month at the lowest price available! Well, that's our offer to you and here's how you benefit by becoming a Regency Romance subscriber:

- **4 FREE Introductory Regency Romances are delivered to your doorstep**
- **4 BRAND NEW Regencies are then delivered each month (usually before they're available in bookstores)**
- **Subscribers save almost $4.00 every month**
- **Home delivery is always FREE**
- **You also receive a FREE monthly newsletter, which features author profiles, discounts, subscriber benefits, book previews and more**
- **No risks or obligations...in other words, you can cancel whenever you wish with no questions asked**

Join the thousands of readers who enjoy the savings and convenience offered to Regency Romance subscribers. After your initial introductory shipment, you receive 4 brand-new Zebra Regency Romances each month to examine for 10 days. Then, if you decide to keep the books, you'll pay the preferred subscriber's price of just $4.00 per title. That's only $16.00 for all 4 books and there's never an extra charge for shipping and handling.

It's a no-lose proposition, so return the FREE BOOK CERTIFICATE today!

Say Yes to 4 Free Books!
Complete and return the order card to receive this $19.96 value, ABSOLUTELY FREE!

FREE BOOK CERTIFICATE

YES! Please rush me 4 Zebra Regency Romances without cost or obligation. I understand that each month thereafter I will be able to preview 4 brand-new Regency Romances FREE for 10 days. Then, if I should decide to keep them, I will pay the money-saving preferred subscriber's price of just $16.00 for all 4...that's a savings of almost $4 off the publisher's price with no additional charge for shipping and handling. I may return any shipment within 10 days and owe nothing, and I may cancel this subscription at any time. My 4 FREE books will be mine to keep in any case.

Name _____

Address _____ Apt. _____

City _____ State _____ Zip _____

Telephone ( ) _____

Signature _____ RN0H0A
(If under 18, parent or guardian must sign.)

Treat yourself to 4 FREE Regency Romances!

IIₒᵣₗᵢᵤₗₗᵤᵤᵢₗₗₗᵢₗₗₗᵤₗₗₗᵤₗₗₗᵤₗₗₗₗₗₗₗₗₗₗₗₗₗₗᵤᵤI

REGENCY ROMANCE BOOK CLUB
Zebra Home Subscription Service, Inc.
P.O. Box 5214
Clifton NJ 07015-5214

PLACE
STAMP
HERE

thew hesitated and made Robert's heart swell by solemnly bowing to Madelyn.

Just as solemnly, Madelyn returned the bow and acknowledged Mary's little farewell wave with a listless movement of her fingers. Matthew grasped the dog's collar and firmly ushered it upstairs.

"I *tried* to catch Matthew," said Melanie, trying to absolve herself from blame when Robert gave her a pointed look. She was still wearing her best blue dress, but the matching ribbons in her hair had come undone and were dragging on her shoulders. "The dog escaped from the nursery, and Matthew—"

"Yes, I *quite* understand," Robert said with a sigh. "You were trying to save Matthew from getting in trouble. If you promise to be very quiet and behave yourself, you may join the ladies in the parlor. I believe Amy and Aggie have been allowed to stay up late as well."

"Thank you, Uncle Robert!" Melanie cried, kissing him enthusiastically on the cheek when he bent down to her. She gave Madelyn a gloating look. The little wretch knew very well that the disturbance had interrupted a tender scene. Robert made a mental note to disabuse Melanie of her flattering but misguided conviction that every female who exchanged a civil word with Robert was determined to trap him into marriage.

Melanie started to run toward the parlor, but she stopped abruptly, gave her uncle a conscience-stricken look over her shoulder, and proceeded in a more decorous manner.

Robert shook his head, but he couldn't help smiling. Melanie was a good girl, too, beneath her tortured adolescent façade. He was still smiling when he reached out his hand, man to man, for Mark's.

"Thank you, Mark. I can't bear to think what

might have happened if you had not been quick
enough to catch your sister," he told his nephew.
"You may join the ladies in the parlor, too, if you
wish. The other gentlemen will be in directly, for
Lord Blakely, it seems, cannot do without the company of his wife for a carouse of any great length."

"Are you coming, too, Uncle Robert?" Mark
asked, looking gratified. "After you read Mary and
Matthew their story, I mean?"

"Later, perhaps," he said with a telltale glance at
Madelyn.

"Oh. All right," Mark said, rolling his eyes in a
droll look of good-natured adolescent scorn at his
uncle's obvious intention of resuming his interrupted dalliance under the mistletoe with Lady
Madelyn. To Robert's relief, the youth obliged his
uncle by not asking any more questions as he made
a hasty departure for the ladies and the dainty pastries that had made Vanessa's cook famous throughout the neighborhood.

Robert attempted to draw Madelyn back into his
arms, but she merely shook her head at him.

"What is wrong, Madelyn?" he asked, surprised by
her reluctance. "You did not seem so unwilling to
indulge me a moment ago."

"A moment ago a herd of animals hadn't converged upon us," she said tartly.

"Madelyn," he said coaxingly. "Where is your
sense of humor? They meant no harm."

"It pleases you to think so," she sniffed in a finick-
ing tone of voice that reminded Robert unpleasantly
of the snooty Lady Letitia. "This is the most intoler-
able household! One cannot hear oneself *think* for
all the noise and interruptions!"

Robert's jaw hardened.

"Your real objection, I gather, is to the presence

of my wards," he said deliberately. "I am sorry their mere existence inconveniences you, Madelyn, but I cannot make them disappear to suit your pleasure."

If she wanted a fight, he was frustrated enough to indulge her. But her ladyship apparently couldn't be bothered to give him the satisfaction of telling her what a spoiled, shallow person she was to resent his orphaned wards.

"It is rather late, Robert," Madelyn said coldly. "I think we have nothing else to say to one another."

"Yes," he said, forcing a polite smile to his lips when his most ardent wish was to take her by her lovely shoulders and shake her until her teeth rattled. "It is rather late, as you say."

Madelyn had almost finished the frustrating task of unhooking the back of her evening gown by herself without tearing the costly fabric when she heard someone rap discreetly on the door to her suite.

Alice, she assumed, come to help her get ready for bed.

"Come," she called out.

The door opened, creaking a little, and she heard someone step inside.

"Do help me get the rest of this gown undone," Madelyn said in some relief. "My poor arms are about to fall off from straining."

Madelyn frowned when no cheerful, willing maid walked into the bedchamber.

Feeling a bit apprehensive, Madelyn stepped cautiously out of the bedchamber and screamed at the top of her lungs.

Cedric Wyndham was standing in her room!

Wide-eyed, she clutched the top half of her gown to her muslin-and-lace-clad bosom. She was uncomfortably aware that these delicate undergarments left little to the imagination.

"I must speak!" he said impetuously, throwing one hand out in appeal.

"Mr. Wyndham!" she breathed, backing away. "You must go away *at once!* What if you are discovered here?"

"I made sure no one saw me, I promise you," he said.

"Are you foxed?" she asked, almost hoping he was. At least that would be a reasonable explanation for his shocking behavior.

Not an *acceptable* explanation but a reasonable one.

"I assure you I have not had one drop of alcohol beyond a glass of wine at dinner," he told her. "Lady Madelyn, you *must* hear me out. I beg of you! I shall go mad if you will not!"

Shockingly, the poor man ran an agitated hand through his hair and rumpled his meticulously styled blond curls. His mouth trembled as if he might burst into tears.

Madelyn averted her face. It was painful to witness such suffering. Perhaps the major part of her attraction for him had not been her fortune, after all.

Maybe, she thought, here was the love she had sought in vain.

A future with Robert Langtry was impossible. Madelyn didn't think she was unselfish enough to share him with those children, not even if they *would* condescend to let him marry her. She couldn't even share a kiss with him under the mistletoe without terrified kittens launching themselves onto his back and big, woolly dogs leading a parade of demanding children into the room to tear him from her arms. Madelyn could hardly wait to marry Robert until the children were grown. By the time that happened, she would be . . . thirty! *No one* was that patient, especially her!

Was it too much to expect a man to love her—and only her—with all his heart? Robert might kiss her with a passion that made her toes curl, but he forgot Madelyn's very existence as soon as his wards appeared on the scene.

It was time for Madelyn to give up that forlorn hope and get on with her life.

She regarded Mr. Wyndham with a kindly eye. His obvious anxiety to marry her was balm to her wounded vanity.

"Lady Madelyn, if you will just hear me out—" he began again, looking worried by her silence. "My happiness depends upon it."

Madelyn bowed her head in acquiescence. She had treated him abominably by leaving him in suspense.

At least if she accepted his proposal she would be making *someone* happy! Mr. Wyndham would make her a charming and devoted husband. Lady Letitia would be thrilled. Madelyn's guardian would approve. The gossips would be silenced forever on the subject of the rich heiress not being able to attach a man.

And she would be able to put Robert Langtry out of her heart and mind at last.

"Yes, Mr. Wyndham," she said softly. "I *will* hear you out, but not now. I shall meet you in the conservatory in ten minutes. We should be quite alone there."

Vanessa's conservatory was the most romantic spot in the house.

Mr. Wyndham's shoulders sagged with relief.

"Thank you, dear lady," he said, gracefully sinking to one knee and kissing her hand in gratitude for her concession. She thought she felt a drop of moisture on the back of her wrist. "I appreciate this more than I can ever express to you."

How chivalrous he is, Madelyn thought, charmed by this romantic gesture. She had not suspected such hidden depths of feeling beneath Mr. Wyndham's façade of worldly sophistication.

Madelyn was very sorry, indeed, that she had been the instrument of his suffering.

But tonight she would make it up to him.

Robert was quite at the other end of the hall on his way back from his wards' bedrooms in the nursery when he heard Madelyn scream. Madelyn's singing voice was so powerful that she could raise it effortlessly to be heard by persons in the back of even the largest room. Its volume was positively earsplitting when she raised it in genuine alarm.

He took off at a run for the source of the sound.

"What in the *hell* is going on here!" Robert demanded as he burst into Madelyn's room. The door screeched on its hinges and slammed against the wall with a reverberating thud.

Robert's vision was clouded by a haze of red-hot anger. When his seething brain registered the fact that Madelyn's gown was half off her body and Wyndham had his filthy hands on her, Robert grabbed Mr. Wyndham by the throat and shook him like the despicable rat he was.

He was about to smash his fist in the blackguard's pretty face when Madelyn's cool voice stopped him dead.

"Release him, if you please, Mr. Langtry," Madelyn said crisply. "I am not in the least danger, I assure you."

"But . . . I heard you scream," he protested.

"A misunderstanding, only. Do let go of Mr. Wyndham. *Now*, if you please."

Robert blinked and focused on her face. Although she was clutching the upper half of her gown to her bosom in a vain attempt at modesty, she wasn't in the least frightened. Irrationally, he was disappointed. He would have dearly loved to plant the fellow a facer.

When Robert's lax fingers released him, Mr. Wyndham gave him a poisonous look and straightened his sleeves.

"Lady Madelyn," Mr. Wyndham said, ignoring Robert as if he were beneath his notice. "Please believe you have my undying admiration and respect. I shall look forward to our meeting."

"I thank you, Mr. Wyndham," Madelyn said with a regal inclination of her head.

Mr. Wyndham gave Robert an ironic bow and went to the door with that prissy, mincing gait of his.

Robert snarled and would have followed.

"Let it go, Robert," she said softly.

Robert looked at Madelyn's beautiful face, and his mouth went dry.

She continued to hold the gown up in front of her to protect her modesty. Even so, Robert was dazzled by the sight of her creamy shoulders revealed above the rich fabric.

He suddenly grasped her bare shoulders. She was so startled that she let the front of the gown fall, revealing her delicately embroidered chemise.

"What have you done, Madelyn?" he demanded. "What is this about a meeting?"

"You are *hurting* me, Mr. Langtry! If you leave bruises on my arms, I am going to give you *such* a clout!"

"*Why*, Madelyn?" he persisted as he removed his hands and clenched them into fists at his side to prevent himself from wrapping them around her pretty neck. She immediately pulled the gown up in front of her again.

"That is none of your business," she snarled. Her eyes were shooting green sparks at him.

"Oh, I see! Pardon *me* for interrupting your sordid little tête-à-tête!"

"*Don't*, Robert," she said, suddenly looking weary.

Robert gave her an ironic little bow.

"I beg pardon for the intrusion, your ladyship," he said sarcastically. "I will remove my offensive self from your presence now, and the next time I hear you scream for help, I shall go about my business and let you scream away."

"Robert, wait," she said hesitantly.

He looked back.

"I seem to be in a bit of difficulty. I know it is not quite the thing to ask, but would you be so kind as to hook up my gown again?"

His jaw dropped.

"No, you must excuse me," he said, certain that touching that perfect, creamy skin would be a grave error of judgment.

"But I have promised to meet Mr. Wyndham in the conservatory in ten minutes, and I shall never get it done up again by myself."

"You want me to hook up your gown so you can meet with your lover?" he asked in disbelief. "That is a trifle insensitive, even for you, my dear."

"Oh, *do* stop being so odious! Would you rather I met him like *this*?"

"No," he said ruefully.

"Then get on with it!" She turned and presented

her smooth, flawless back with a touching, if mis-guided, confidence in his self-control.

Robert took a gulp of air to steady his rioting senses and obeyed. Her skin flushed and warmed as he inadvertently touched it with fingers made clumsy by his attempt to maintain as little flesh-on-flesh contact as possible.

"I am much obliged to you," she said with a little catch in her voice when he had finished.

"Always happy to be of service," he said dryly.

Then he quickly got out of the room before she could see how badly his hands were shaking.

Eight

Robert could have taught the early Christian martyrs a thing or two when it came to torturing himself over Lady Madelyn, so he skulked in the shadows outside the entrance to the conservatory with some vague notion of stopping her from meeting with Mr. Wyndham.

When he peered into the slightly moist, glass-fronted doors at the hothouse flowers within, though, he could see the fellow anxiously pacing before a statue of Diana the Huntress surrounded by the yellow roses and purple irises that were Vanessa's pride and joy.

The fellow had gone to some pains to set his scene, Robert thought sourly. He had lighted the candles set in holders at intervals along the paths through this extravagant indoor garden, so the flowers were illuminated with a soft glow, and having stripped off his coat, he was clad in flowing shirtsleeves with his collar opened to reveal his strong throat. He was the very picture of the distraught lover, going mad from passion.

No woman could refuse the man who proposed to her in such a romantic spot, Robert thought in despair. Especially not the volatile and impulsive Lady Madelyn.

He badly wanted to relieve his frustration by stalking into the room and drawing Wyndham's claret, but reason intervened. If he intruded, the lovers would only meet somewhere else. While he hesitated, wondering what to do next, Madelyn walked right by him and went into the conservatory with a purposeful step. She looked rather too much like a woman who had already made up her mind for Robert's comfort. Mercifully, she hadn't seen him in the shadows.

He should go away now and save himself the pain of seeing her rush into Wyndham's arms, but he was mesmerized by the way the candlelight turned her hair into burnished copper and glimmered along the rich emerald fabric of her gown as she approached Wyndham.

Instead, he watched. And suffered. He couldn't hear what Wyndham was saying, but he didn't need to. His worst nightmare unfolded like a dumb-play before his eyes.

Wyndham grasped both of Madelyn's hands in his and blurted out what was no doubt some florid, impassioned declaration of his undying love and devotion. Madelyn had her back to Robert, so he couldn't see the expression on her face. But he could tell she was listening intently, and then, to Robert's despair, she nodded in assent.

Wyndham cast himself at her feet and covered her hands with passionate kisses.

The fellow's valet must have the devil's own time keeping his clothes in order the way he was forever rolling around on the floor to impress some woman.

Madelyn kissed her cavalier on the cheek when he rose, and he rushed from the conservatory.

Robert concealed himself in the shadows just in time to avoid being discovered. The look of joy on Wyndham's face told its own tale.

Madelyn, by this time, had seated herself on the stone bench before the statue, picked a yellow rose from a bush, and was twirling it slowly in one hand.

Much against his better judgment, Robert strode into the conservatory, reached down to grasp her arm, and yanked her off the bench to face him.

"What have you done, Madelyn?" he demanded, just as if he didn't know.

She favored him with a brittle smile.

"I've made Mr. Wyndham the happiest of men, obviously," she said with a sardonic jerk of her head toward the door through which the besotted gentleman had passed.

"You cannot marry him," Robert said.

At that she gave a half-hysterical little laugh.

"He will make the announcement to the company in a moment," she said, her voice curiously absent of inflection. She took his arm. "They will think it very strange if I am not present. We had better join them."

"I don't want to hear the bloody announcement," he said, giving her an incredulous look as he flinched away from her. Did she think he was made of stone?

"Oh, I think you should," Madelyn said grimly. "In fact, I insist upon it."

With that, she seized his arm again and marched him out of the room. Heaven help him, Robert made no resistance. He felt as if he were in the grip of a nightmare.

They arrived in the drawing room to find that Mr. Wyndham wasn't there.

Robert looked around, puzzled, but Madelyn gave him an urgent shake of her head when he opened his mouth to speak. He tried to stand apart from Madelyn, but she increased her grip on his arm.

Their hostess gave them a smile of welcome and lifted her teapot with a polite, questioning look on her face to avoid interrupting the conversation in progress. Madelyn shook her head.

Just then, Mr. Wyndham escorted a radiant Pamela Crowley into the room. Her sleepy little girls, still in their nightgowns and holding on to Wyndham's neck as if they were afraid he might get away, were perched one in each of his arms.

Robert glanced quickly at Madelyn, but she was staring straight ahead with an inscrutable look on her face.

"Ladies and gentlemen, I am delighted to announce that Mrs. Crowley has done me the very great honor of consenting to be my wife," Wyndham declared. As the others expressed amazement and bewildered good wishes, he placed a tender kiss on his prospective bride's lips.

Pamela Crowley obviously was ecstatic, as well she *should* be at having the good fortune to attract such an eligible fiancé. Robert did not miss the gloating expression of triumph she cast in Madelyn's direction.

Lady Letitia gave a theatrical gasp and directed a glare at the happy future bridegroom that should have felled him where he stood. The earl gave him a look of utter contempt. Alexander's expression was filled with compassion as he looked at Madelyn. Robert's mother was obviously furious at what she no doubt thought of as Mrs. Crowley's betrayal of her trust, and she gave Robert and Madelyn both a stare of outrage that made it difficult to see which one of them she blamed more for this unwelcome development. Everyone else watched Madelyn avidly for her reaction.

Madelyn proved her talent as an actress by calmly

smiling back at the sea of eyes fixed upon her for some sign of mental anguish.

"I wish you happy, Mrs. Crowley," Madelyn said, kissing Pamela on the cheek. The bride-to-be was watching Madelyn carefully, as if she might still step forward to snatch Mr. Wyndham from her grasp, when Madelyn turned to congratulate her former suitor.

"But—" began Robert when Madelyn slipped back beside him.

"Mr. Wyndham has the highest standards of propriety," she said quietly as she continued to maintain a false, sweet smile on her lips for the benefit of their company. Robert didn't miss the little catch in her voice. "He could not in all conscience offer for Mrs. Crowley until he first withdrew his offer for my hand. It argues for a certain amount of sensitivity on Mr. Wyndham's part."

"He is an idiot," Robert said, trying without success to hide his relief.

"How happy he looks," Madelyn observed wryly. "He certainly was never in such alt at the prospect of marrying *me*. And here was I, thinking he meant to lay his heart at my feet. I am persuaded this must give you great satisfaction, Mr. Langtry."

"Robert. Please. I hope you know it could never give me satisfaction to see you hurt," he said gently. "My poor dear."

"Blast it, Robert," she said through her smiling teeth. "This is *not* the time to be kind to me."

Lady Letitia sailed up to Madelyn and put a consoling arm around her shoulders to effectively separate Madelyn from Robert. She whispered urgently at Madelyn, casting scornful little sneers at Mr. Wyndham all the while.

"Yes. Quite delightful news, is it not?" he heard

Madelyn say quite deliberately in response to Lady Letitia's hissing complaints.

Madelyn might be putting on a brave front, but Robert could see that Wyndham's defection had damaged her pride. He had not missed Mrs. Whittaker's maliciously gleeful look in Madelyn's direction. She would be pleased to see the proud heiress humbled, if only to spite Lady Letitia, whose mind had been so set on a match between Madelyn and Mr. Wyndham. Lady Letitia had been quite liberal with her snubs in the Whittakers' direction over the years.

The whole scene, in Robert's opinion, was unbelievably awkward, and he started to inch toward the door preparatory to making his escape from it.

A glance back at where Lady Madelyn, now abandoned even by Lady Letitia, stood all alone with a forced smile on her face had him retracing his steps.

If ever Madelyn needed a friend, it was now.

"Wait until she gets her hands on him," he whispered into Madelyn's ear when she gave him a surprised and grateful look. "The man will be under the cat's paw for the rest of his life."

"Robert," she said in reproof, but she smiled at him. Robert accepted two glasses of champagne from the servant circulating with a tray. He handed one to Madelyn.

"Let us drink to it, shall we?" Robert said with a wink as he touched his glass to hers.

The next day, Lady Madelyn kept to her room and refused to see anyone on the pretext of preparing for her journey.

Robert, heavily engaged in preparations for his

family's return to Yorkshire, honored her wishes and did not try to see her.

What was left for him to say to her, after all?

"Poor Robert," said Mrs. Whittaker sympathetically when he entered the dining room. She had known him since he was in short coats, so he could hardly expect her to respect his privacy. She patted his shoulder. "How *could* Pamela Crowley have used you so!"

He looked at her blankly for a moment. His head was so full of Madelyn that he had forgotten all about the plot to pair him with Mrs. Crowley.

"There was no formal understanding between us," he said with a shrug. "Mrs. Crowley is free to marry whomever she wishes."

"She's a heartless hussy," Mrs. Whittaker insisted after she had followed him all along the row of chafing dishes and planted herself at his side at the table, murmuring words of comfort all along the way. "She had us all fooled, but she was wrong for you. Now, my Mary Ann . . ."

Robert choked on the coffee he had raised to his lips.

Mary Ann! He might have known that Mrs. Whittaker, a meddler of the highest order and the mother of three unmarried daughters, would be quick to suggest an alternate wife. To Robert's alarm, Mrs. Whittaker raised one imperious hand to summon her vivacious nineteen-year-old daughter to her side.

Robert was searching his mind for a polite way to voice his objections to having another prospective bride thrust upon him when Mrs. Whittaker bid her daughter to keep Robert company and sailed away, looking well pleased with herself.

"Mary Ann, I, ah—"

The girl burst into laughter.

"Do not look so hunted, Robert, dear," she said with the frank familiarity of a girl he had watched grow from an awkward adolescent into a confident young woman. Her pretty brown eyes were sparkling with amusement. "You are much too old and dull for me, and so I told my mother last night when she hatched this precious scheme."

"What a dreadful girl you are," he said fondly.

He frowned when he saw his mother seat herself farther down the table near Mrs. Whittaker for what appeared to be a comfortable coze. Wonderful. They probably were making his and Mary Ann's wedding arrangements.

"Why is Mother not wearing her traveling dress?" he wondered aloud. "She knows I mean to leave for Yorkshire after breakfast."

"Did she not tell you? She is not going home with you."

Robert stared at her.

"What are you talking about, Mary Ann? Of course she is going home with us."

"Ah, she *hasn't* told you." Robert thought Mary Ann looked quite unpardonably cheerful at the prospect of enlightening him. "Mr. Wyndham and Mrs. Crowley begged her to accompany them to his father's estate to ask his support of the match. Unless Lord Barlowe approves of Mrs. Crowley, Mr. Wyndham could very well find himself disinherited. They need a respectable lady along to preserve her reputation on the journey or all is lost."

"But . . . last night my mother called Mrs. Crowley—"

"Let me guess! A back-stabbing sneak thief who has betrayed her friendship to get an introduction to Lord Blakely's party and dash all her hopes of getting a proper wife for you?" Mary Ann supplied helpfully. "And she will never trust the heartless hussy again as long as she lives?"

"She did say something of the sort, yes," Robert admitted.

"It seems our Pamela quite melted her heart by saying that she is the only one she can turn to in her hour of need."

"So much for family loyalty," he said grimly. "No matter. The children and I shall get along perfectly well without her, although it will be hard to explain why their grandmother may not spend Christmas with them."

He gulped down the rest of his breakfast, nodded politely to Mary Ann, and bore down on his mother.

"We will see you at home," Mrs. Whittaker said gaily to him when he approached the two older ladies. "Perhaps we will have a ball next month." Her speculative gaze lit on Mary Ann, who had followed him and seated herself on her mother's other side. "For the young people." She simpered at Robert.

"That would be lovely, Mrs. Whittaker," Robert said through gritted teeth. "A word with you in private, if you please, Mother."

"I swear I would have not known Mary Ann," Mrs. Langtry said brightly to Robert when she took his arm and permitted him to escort her from the room. "She is grown so lovely this past year, is she not?"

"Yes. Fortunately, she thinks I am much too old and dull for her, and there's an end to the matter," he said with mean satisfaction.

Mrs. Langtry's mouth dropped open.

"She never said that!" she exclaimed indignantly.

"You know Mary Ann, Mother. Of *course* she did. The girl's a great gun. Now, enough of that nonsense. What did you mean by agreeing to act as Mrs. Crowley's duenna?"

"That Pamela Crowley is a back-stabbing, scheming, ungrateful hussy," Mrs. Langtry said with a sigh. "But she needs my help, and I hope I am too good a Christian to deny her." She gave Robert a stern look. "Not that she is *entirely* to blame for what happened. A widow with small children to rear alone has to look out for herself, after all."

"I know," Robert acknowledged glumly. His mother had made it quite clear that if he had paid more attention to Mrs. Crowley, she wouldn't have taken a second look at that tallow-headed fop. "But how are you to get home?"

"Pamela and her girls must return to Yorkshire to close down their house, so I shall go with them," she said. "The poor woman has no mother to help her, for her parents washed their hands of her when she married Mr. Crowley. They must be *dreadful* people. Did I tell you what her father wrote to her when she informed him of Laura's birth?"

"He had no further interest in her or any of the mongrels she might breed with that impecunious, mealymouthed cleric she had defied him to marry," Robert said impatiently, having heard this story many times.

"Just so!" her mother said indignantly. "I will just come with you to explain to the children."

"They will find it difficult to understand why you are not going to spend Christmas with us," he pointed out.

She gave a wistful little sigh.

"Robert, darling," she said, touching his cheek in a bid for understanding. "I lead such a dull life in the country with you and the children. Can you blame me for wanting a little excitement?"

He could, and did. She had never expressed the slightest wish for excitement before. But he was determined to accept her defection with good grace rather than embark upon a pointless argument with her. She always seemed to win them, anyway.

At least he would be spared his mother's reproaches for not proposing to Mrs. Crowley himself all the way to Yorkshire.

"There will be many more Christmases, after all," she said cheerfully.

Robert could tell she was already relishing her important role as the heroine and savior of a pair of young lovers.

"I didn't get to say good-bye to Lady Madelyn!" protested Mary when Mrs. Langtry dutifully had kissed each of her grandchildren and Robert guided them toward the coach drawn up in front of the manor.

"Lady Madelyn!" Melanie scoffed. "Do you think she gives the snap of her fingers about *you?*"

Robert gave Melanie a quelling look and put a sympathetic hand on Mary's shoulder.

"I wanted to tell her good-bye," Mary said. Her little face crumpled. "And now I will never see her again."

"I'm sorry, love," Robert said sympathetically as he helped her into the carriage.

He knew just how she felt.

Vanessa and Alexander came outside to see them off.

"Are you certain you will not stay another night?" Vanessa asked politely. "The weather seems to have grown worse."

Indeed, the day was gray, and it had begun to snow again.

"No, I thank you, Vanessa," Robert said, patting Matthew on the head when he gave his uncle a heart-rending look of appeal. Much as his wards enjoyed the companionship of the other children in Lord Blakely's family, he could not in good conscience inflict his family on his hosts any longer. Fortunately, his nieces and nephews were fond of a journey and quite delighted in stopping at inns along the way. Once the nursery dog was out of sight, Matthew would regain his enthusiasm for the trip, Robert knew. "If we make good time, we will arrive at the first inn by dark, and that will be sufficient progress for today."

"Well, take care, then," Alexander said jovially. He was not quite so adept as his wife at disguising his eagerness to bid his guests farewell.

They were on the road for some hours when a swift black coach overtook them.

"It's Lady Madelyn!" Mary said, waving frantically through the window.

"You said that when the last coach passed, but it was only an old man," scoffed Melanie.

This time Mary happened to be correct. Robert looked out the window over Mary's bobbing head in time to see Madelyn wave back at Mary through the coach's window as both vehicles slowed to allow Madelyn's to pass safely on the narrow, slippery road. The snow was still falling unabated.

"I will have Jimmy stop for the night at the next inn we pass," Robert said, estimating that it would start to grow dark within the hour.

"Maybe Lady Madelyn will stay at the same inn tonight," Mary suggested hopefully.

"I don't think so, sweetheart. She might change her horses at the inn and perhaps have dinner there, but then she'll drive straight through the night to her destination."

"That's what rich people do," Matthew said knowingly.

At that moment Robert gave a startled exclamation as a stagecoach careened around them at breakneck speed. Gaily decorated with mistletoe on the doors, the vehicle was crammed with people both inside and on the roof. From the way the thing was weaving, Robert guessed that some drunken fool had bribed the coachman to let him drive the team of horses as a lark. Robert's coachman sharply drew the Langtrys' coach to the side of the road in order to avoid disaster.

Even the usually intrepid Melanie held a shaking hand to her heart. The two younger children had squealed in alarm and buried their faces in Robert's shoulders.

"There, there. We're safe," he crooned to them. Then he added in a stronger voice, "No thanks to that bloody *idiot!*"

"*Language*, Uncle Robert," Mark said impudently.

An hour later, the bend in the road revealed a terrible sight. The same stagecoach was tipped over on its side, and people were milling about, trying to help the injured passengers. The black coach with which it had collided was half in a ditch.

Madelyn!

With his heart in his throat, Robert ordered his coachman to stop.

"Don't look out the windows no matter what you hear," he admonished his wards before he leapt out of the coach. When Mark would have followed him, he pushed him back with a curt "Mark! Stay here!"

Robert's stomach lurched at the sight of several inert bodies lying on the road with other people tending them. They looked like so many broken dolls. He prayed that Matthew and Mary, at least, obeyed his order not to look. The sickly pale goose and turkey carcasses hanging off the sides of the gaily decorated public stagecoach in anticipation of Christmas and the rosettes decorating the frightened horses added a macabre touch to the scene.

"Where are the occupants of this coach?" he cried out when he looked in the window of the black vehicle and found it empty. Lady Madelyn's trunks were lying about all smashed, their expensive contents strewn about in the drifting snow.

A middle-aged man, obviously a doctor from the worn leather bag at his side and his competence in bandaging the injured man lying on the ground before him, looked up at Robert.

"I have the guard here," he said. "His mistress is over there with the others."

Robert caught a flash of green fabric the color of Madelyn's traveling costume from the corner of his eye, and his heart sank when he saw it covering the unmoving body of a woman.

"Madelyn!" he shouted in alarm as he ran forward.

To his relief, Madelyn looked up quickly from where she was bending over the green-clad body.

"Robert! Oh, *Robert!*" Madelyn cried, looking glad to see him. She apparently had used her own coat to cover the woman lying in front of her. The injured woman stirred and started to moan. "Help me with Alice. I think she's broken her arm. *Careful,* now!"

"I've got her," Robert said, bending to scoop the maid up in his arms.

The doctor approached, and Madelyn called out to him.

"How is John?" she asked anxiously. "And Sammy?"

"Your Sammy will be well enough. Just a nasty knock on the head, but I'll want to keep watch on him for a time," the doctor said. "John is your guard?" Madelyn nodded solemnly. "I will need to take him to my surgery. Don't look so worried, miss. He'll come through the business right enough."

"Oh, thank heaven," Madelyn said devoutly.

"Here, young fella," the doctor said to Robert. "I will take the injured people to my surgery in my carriage. You must take this lady and some of the other uninjured female passengers to the inn before they freeze to death in this weather."

"But I—"

"I'll just have a look at the young woman you have there," he said, indicating Alice. "Here, my girl, you can walk. You are more frightened than hurt," he added with a rough kindness.

Robert carefully lowered Alice to her feet, and she clung to the doctor with her good arm.

"That's a good girl," the doctor said, giving the injured arm an expert look. "Broke your wing, I see, little bird."

"But we can't just leave Alice," Madelyn protested. "I'm *responsible* for her!"

"She'll be better off with me," the doctor assured her. "I'll have to set her arm for her if she doesn't want it to mend crooked."

The girl gave a little moan of distress, and the doctor patted her good arm reassuringly.

"Alice is a member of Lord Blakely's household," Robert said. "I must make arrangements to have her conveyed to his estate when she is well enough to travel."

"Certainly," he said. "The inn is a mile up the road. I will call on you there after I treat these patients in my surgery. If you can drive your own coach, I'd be grateful if you would have your coachman come with me. I could use a strong young fellow to help me move the injured."

"I can drive it," Robert said, feeling overcome. There were only four female passengers, including Madelyn, who were unhurt. But no one was dead, thank God. Robert helped his new passengers into the coach, and although it was a squeeze, they managed to make room for everyone by having Madelyn hold Mary in her lap while Mark held Matthew. Fortunately, another passing carriage had stopped to help and would take some of the men.

"Thank you, sir, for stopping to help us," said one tearful old woman.

"Not at all," Robert said, patting her shoulder as he closed the door and leapt up to the bench.

Their progress to the inn was slow despite Robert's urgency to arrive before dark. Robert hadn't driven a vehicle so large for a long time, although, like many aspiring town beaux, he often had done so for entertainment as a younger man.

Those carefree days seemed very far away now.

Once the coach was set in motion, Madelyn kept up a flow of social conversation with the stagecoach passengers to try to lighten the mood. They had just been through a harrowing experience, and they were quick to respond to any overtures of friendliness.

The travelers even managed to smile and make jokes at intervals, they were so glad to have been transferred from the raw wind to a comfortable—if crowded—coach.

Madelyn's social acumen rarely failed to come to her aid, she thought complacently.

Mary was shaking and clinging to Madelyn like a monkey. Matthew was clinging to Mark in a similar manner. Melanie's face was positively ashen. It was then that Madelyn realized how upset the children must be.

Their parents had died in a carriage accident.

How *could* Madelyn have been so stupid?

Her attempts at cheerful conversation must seem about as appropriate to them as laughter at a funeral.

Until Madelyn met Robert's wards, she had thought of herself as a good person.

Was she not accepted everywhere and invited to all the best parties? Did she not strive to be a kind and generous mistress to her employees?

But three years ago, when she met Robert's wards, she had to revise her own favorable opinion of herself.

They had not liked her. Period. It was obvious from the way their eyes narrowed the first time they saw her.

Her self-esteem suffered a plunge to the depths of despair.

It was bad enough to lose Robert.

It was even worse to discover she was the kind of person that small children detested on sight.

Maturity brought new insight. They had been afraid of losing their uncle to her. They thought she would make Robert send them away if she married him. They were just children, after all, and not the malignant creatures they had seemed to her at the time.

How could they know she was every bit as much afraid of them? They could take Robert away from *her.*

And they did.

It should have been some consolation that Mary and Matthew seemed to like her now, but they, she suspected, merely thought she was like their mother.

Well, she wasn't.

She didn't know *anything* about children, and her insensitivity in behaving as if a carriage accident were nothing more than a new social experience proved it.

If Mary and Matthew were fooled, their sister Melanie knew the truth. She had given Madelyn a look of such hostility when she got into the carriage that Madelyn almost recoiled.

"You're only being nice to us because you want to marry Uncle Robert," the girl had said.

Oh, Melanie. If only it were that simple.

"Lady Madelyn, are you going to travel all the way home with us?" Mary asked wistfully.

Bless Mary.

Madelyn couldn't help giving her an affectionate squeeze.

The poor little thing didn't realize Madelyn was the last person in the world to give a child comfort. She simply did not have the knack.

"I probably will wait until my carriage can be repaired and resume my journey with a hired driver and guard," she said.

She didn't miss Melanie's look of relief.

Once they were at the inn, Robert dispatched a messenger to Lord Blakely's estate to give Alexander a report on what happened to Alice. It was Madelyn's place, not Robert's, to be responsible for the maidservant who accompanied her, but Mary refused to be separated from Madelyn.

Melanie gave her sister a look of withering disgust as she sat with them in the reception room of the hotel to wait for Robert to bespeak supper and engage rooms for them.

Madelyn was horrified to find that there were only a few rooms available at the inn for the night and the landlord was arbitrarily assigning perfect strangers to share rooms with other strangers of the appropriate sex. Robert had managed to procure one of the larger rooms for himself and his wards, but no other single rooms were available. Robert generously offered Madelyn a place with them, a courtesy that Melanie seconded with a resentful glare.

"You are very kind, but I would not wish to impose on you and the children," Madelyn said politely. Besides, she could hardly sleep in the same room as Robert! What was he thinking?

Instead, she agreed to share a room with the two most respectable looking female passengers from the stagecoach. They were simple countrywomen, a mother and daughter, and they were pathetically grateful when Madelyn insisted on paying for the entire room in advance instead of sharing the cost with them. They had not brought much money, the mother confided, because they had expected to drive straight through to their village on the stagecoach without stopping anywhere for the night.

With a glimmer of grim humor, Madelyn conjured up a vision of what her guardian, Mr. Kenniston, would think of such an arrangement. That gentleman had been relentless in his zeal to make sure his charge was protected from contamination by socially inferior persons, evidently in the belief that those who practiced indifferent hygiene could transmit illnesses to those more delicately bred.

Mr. Kenniston was obliged to keep the heiress in good health because the well-being of Madelyn's estates and all the souls who depended upon them for employment would be jeopardized if anything should happen to her.

Madelyn had never flattered herself that affection for *her* had anything to do with the meticulous performance of Mr. Kenniston's responsibilities to her.

Even so, she hoped he never learned of this day's work. He was getting quite old, and she had to admit he had dedicated his life to his ward's interests for the past several years.

One of the reasons Madelyn had returned to England so unexpectedly was her cousin Elizabeth's letter, which described Mr. Kenniston's health as failing.

This was something else for Madelyn to feel guilty about. If she had not been gadding about the Continent in a vain attempt to get over her doomed infatuation with Robert Langtry, poor Mr. Kenniston possibly would not have had to deplete so much of his energy in managing her affairs.

Madelyn smiled at the elderly countrywoman and her middle-aged daughter to put them at ease. They obviously were flustered by the prospect of sharing a room with a lady of such obvious quality.

Madelyn's heart sank when she saw the room, but one look at her companions' faces made her clamp her lips down hard on her exclamation of dismay.

Alone with her maid, she would have instantly demanded another, but her companions were regarding the shabby room as if it were an agreeable surprise. Madelyn realized that for them it obviously represented lavish accommodations.

"A fire," one of them said, crossing the room quickly to warm her hands as soon as the landlord left with a promise of dinner. Her tired eyes shone with tears of relief. "And supper brought to the room as if we were quality. If you had not agreed to share with us, we would have been given a much worse place to spend the night, I can promise you!"

Madelyn would have been hard put to imagine a worse place than this dark, cramped little room, but it would have been churlish to say as much, so she merely smiled.

"You will have the bed, of course, my lady," the elderly countrywoman said, indicating a bed that was much smaller than any of those Madelyn had occupied alone since she was a child. "Betsy and I will be warm as toast on the floor by the fire if the landlord will give us a few blankets."

"Nonsense! The two of you will share the bed," Madelyn said, forcing resolution into her voice. "*I* will sleep on the floor. I am the youngest, after all."

She preferred it, actually, for the floor looked infinitely cleaner than the bed, and she suspected the sheets were far from dry. This was not a luxurious posting inn like those to which she was accustomed, and in her opinion the amenities were abysmal. But Madelyn was determined not to make a fuss about it.

"No, my lady. It ain't fitting!" the middle-aged woman said in astonishment.

"But it is perfectly sensible," Madelyn insisted.

"Well, my old joints aren't what they used to be with all this cold," the elderly woman said, beaming gratefully at Madelyn. "You're a kind lady, and no mistake."

No, I'm not, Madelyn said ruefully to herself.

Nine

Madelyn had never slept on a floor in her life.

If she had, she might not have been so blithe about insisting upon it the night before, she thought as she painfully stretched out her stiff and creaking limbs.

This probably was what being elderly felt like. If so, she wanted no part of it.

One glance at the women peacefully sleeping on the bed was enough to mollify her, however. To Madelyn, the bed looked lumpy, dirty, and uncomfortable. To them, apparently, it was heaven.

The younger countrywoman yawned and sat up when a servant rapped on the door and brought in a ewer and bowl of water.

"It's warm," the woman said in wonder after Madelyn had washed her face and hands, and she picked up the bowl and stuck her finger in it.

Madelyn could not help giving her a quizzical look.

"So I should hope," she said.

"Mother! They have brought us *hot* water to wash in!"

"You're dreaming," the elderly woman said with a nasal snort as she sat up. She gave her daughter a skeptical look and dipped her fingertips into the bowl. She drew her fingers out again and stared at the water as if it had burned her, although it was positively tepid by Madelyn's standards. "It's a miracle!"

With every appearance of enjoyment, the women performed their ablutions with the used water. Madelyn had assumed more water would be coming for the other women, but they apparently knew better.

Apparently poorer people thought nothing of sharing wash water, Madelyn surmised, determined not to let her dismay show. She certainly had no cause for complaint, since she got to use the water first.

She sighed and could actually see her breath. Madelyn was glad she had slept in her clothes; not that she had any choice. She thought wistfully of her three smashed trunks of clothing that were probably still littering the site of the accident. She folded her arms in front of her for warmth and wished she still had her coat, but she could not regret giving it to Alice. Poor girl. Madelyn felt terrible about her injury. She hoped Alice was not in very much pain. And she must discover the whereabouts and conditions of her guard and coachman.

"Thank you for sharing your room with me," Madelyn said politely to the women as she prepared to leave the room. "I must find Mr. Langtry and thank him for his assistance before he continues on his journey with his family."

"Thank *you*, Lady Madelyn," the older woman said with a sigh of real gratitude as she dried off her hands on a towel. "For everything."

For everything. The use of a lumpy bed and her discarded wash water. Madelyn had not met anyone as easy to please as these countrywomen in years. It was rather refreshing.

She was still smiling to herself when she came face-to-face with Robert.

"Mr. Langtry!" she said, trembling a little when his hands rested on her shoulders.

"You are as cold as ice," he said, disconcerting Madelyn by absently chafing some warmth into her frigid arms. His blue eyes were gentle with concern. "I hope you were not too uncomfortable last night."

To her annoyance, Madelyn could feel herself flush hotly. All he had to do was *touch* her and she completely lost the thread of what she started to say.

"Thank you, Mr. Langtry," she said, stepping back to keep herself from burrowing into his arms. "The room was quite adequate."

"Are we back to that 'Mr. Langtry' business again?" he asked quizzically.

"Robert," Madelyn said, taking quite disproportionate pleasure from the sound of his name on her lips.

"That's better," he said with an approving smile as he swiftly removed his coat and gallantly placed it around Madelyn's shoulders. "My coachman returned late in the night with news. Alice's arm *is* broken, but it was a clean break and should mend quickly, fortunately. I am sorry I did not think to inquire as to the whereabouts of your coat."

"It probably isn't fit to be seen in after what it has been through, so Alice may have it with my goodwill, if she wants the thing," Madelyn said, enjoying the comfort of his coat, still warm from his body. It smelled of bay rum and something a bit earthier, like leather or horse. "If you will excuse me, I shall have to find out how long it will take to repair my carriage. If it is beyond a day or two, I will hire another one to convey me to my cousin's house. And I must find

John and Sammy and see if they are well enough to travel."

Robert gave her an incredulous look.

"You cannot think I would leave you here alone to deal with these things by yourself! You are going to Yorkshire with us, of course. I will be happy to convey you to your cousin's house."

"Oh, I could not impose—" she began.

"Madelyn, you have no choice. Your maid is injured, and you can hardly travel unaccompanied. I have already made arrangements for your carriage to be repaired. Fortunately, neither of your men is badly injured, although they will not be able to resume their usual duties for at least a week, the doctor said. My coachman will stay behind and bring them to you in Yorkshire along with your carriage. Your men are looking quite forward to being passengers while Jimmy drives them in state."

She had to smile at that.

"You will be happy to know that Jimmy has managed to retrieve one of your trunks," Robert continued.

"Bless you, Robert!" she exclaimed. "I was afraid I would have to spend the next few weeks in these clothes! I don't know how to thank you for your kindness."

"It is my pleasure," he said, looking a bit embarrassed. "Madelyn, will you speak to Mary? The shock of her parents' deaths in the carriage accident still haunts her, I'm afraid, and despite my reassurances, she thinks you may be dead because you did not spend the night with us."

"How dreadful! Why did you not come for me at once?"

He shrugged.

"I was not sure you would care to be disturbed at

so late an hour. You made it quite clear that you had endured enough of our company for one night."

"Not *care?*" Madelyn was absolutely mortified that he could think her such a monster. "Robert, I did not stay with you last night merely because I did not want to inconvenience you and the children—"

"—and put yourself under a crushing obligation to me," Robert interrupted. "I hope you know by now that I would never presume to take advantage of circumstances—"

"Certainly not," Madelyn said quickly to prevent him from developing that particular theme. "I will speak with Mary at once if you will take me to her."

Robert nodded and took Madelyn's elbow to escort her down the hall in the direction from which he had come.

"Lady Madelyn," shrieked Mary as soon as Mark opened the door to them.

The child burst into tears of relief and pelted straight into Madelyn's waiting arms with such force that Robert had to brace Madelyn's shoulders to keep her from toppling over.

"There, there, my dear," Madelyn said soothingly as she kissed Mary's cheek and smoothed her hair back from her face. "I am much obliged to you for your concern, darling, but I am quite safe, I promise you."

"Where *were* you?" Mary asked, her voice hoarse from weeping. "Why did you not spend the night with us?"

"This room would have been much too small for all of us. I spent the night with a mother and daughter from the stagecoach."

"We are about to go to breakfast," Robert said, patting Mary on the head. "You will join us, will you not, Lady Madelyn? There are no private parlors available, I'm afraid. We shall have to go into the public room."

"I should be delighted to join you," Madelyn said, smiling at him. She wiped Mary's eyes with her finger and stood up with her little hand in hers. "Suddenly I am famished!"

They set off for Yorkshire a bit before noon, after Robert arranged for Jimmy to drive Alice to Lord Blakely's estate in a hired gig. The girl was pathetically grateful when Madelyn insisted she keep her green velvet coat, because Alice's had been torn and muddied in the accident.

By then Madelyn had received possession of her trunk, which was a bit dented but, thankfully, had not opened in the collision.

"Oh, how lovely," she said with a rueful laugh when she opened it. "My evening gowns and jewels. Not very practical attire, I'm afraid, when one is traveling in winter, but better than nothing. At least this cloak will be warm enough if I don't get it wet."

It was with an odd sense of regret that she exchanged Robert's wool coat for the magnificent cobalt-blue velvet cloak lined with fur. It had a hood that Madelyn could pull up around her head and ears for warmth. How odd she would look! Lady Letitia would swoon with shock if she could see her wearing an obvious evening garment over her rumpled traveling clothes.

"Poor girl," Madelyn said apologetically to Alice when Jimmy brought her from the doctor's house. "I feel terrible about your arm. If you had not pushed me to the floor and protected me with your own body, I would not have escaped injury."

"I'm quite all right, my lady," the girl said cheerfully as she pocketed the generous tip Madelyn un-obtrusively slipped to her. "It's been a right adventure. When we're all sitting in the room, I'll have something to say for myself, for a change."

"Ah, the resilience of youth," Robert said with a smile as Jimmy, his coachman, tenderly handed Alice into the gig for the trip to Lord Blakely's estate. Once again, Robert would be driving his own coach.

He extended his arm to Madelyn.

"Shall we, my dear?"

"Indeed, Mr. Langtry," she said, accepting his assistance into the coach. She found herself sand-wiched on one side of the coach between Matthew and Mary, while Mark and Melanie occupied the other side. Fortunately, the Langtrys did not believe in traveling with an excess of either servants or luggage.

"We will have to make shift for ourselves when we get home," Robert said, smiling at the children. "We gave most of the servants leave for Christmas because we expected to stay until New Year's with Vanessa and Alexander. The arrival of Mr. Quentin Alexander Whittaker certainly put paid to those plans!"

He sounded quite cheerful about it. No doubt he was looking forward to being rid of all the match-making mamas and spending the next few weeks in peace before his own hearth—even if it meant he would spend the rest of their journey out in the weather.

By Christmas, Madelyn would be cozily installed with Elizabeth in her comfortable house. She trusted the letter she sent from Lord Blakely's estate would reach her cousin before her actual arrival and hoped Elizabeth would not find it too inconvenient to put up with her for longer than she had planned. Made-lyn made a mental note to arrange for extra food to be brought in. Her hostess was not wealthy by any means.

It seemed Madelyn was always putting someone out, even though she had not intended to.

When Robert closed the door and assumed his perch behind the horses, Madelyn felt a moment of panic.

He was shutting her in *alone* with the children! She needn't have worried, though. Mary and Matthew seemed to accept her presence easily. Mark mainly looked out the window. Melanie scowled at her but remained silent, so it was easy to ignore her.

When they had traveled several miles, it began to snow again.

"How pretty it is," she said, helping Mary draw pictures in the fogged window. Melanie rolled her eyes in scorn at the two of them. Mary had clung to Madelyn's hand through the whole journey, and Madelyn found she enjoyed the adoration in the child's eyes entirely too much.

The snow continued for the next few hours, blanketing the countryside with big, fluffy flakes.

While Mary and Matthew regarded the fall of snow with bright-eyed appreciation, Mark and Melanie exchanged worried glances.

Mark finally reached across Madelyn to touch Mary's forehead. He looked alarmed and rapped on the roof of the carriage to signal Robert. When the coach stopped, he went out to have a whispered conference with his uncle.

"Mary, love," Robert said gently when he came inside the coach and crouched down next to the child. "Are you feeling all right?"

Madelyn gave him a look of inquiry, and then comprehension dawned.

What Madelyn in her ignorance of children took

for bright-eyed interest was no such thing. She touched the little girl's face and was rewarded with an adoring look. Mary's eyes were rimmed with pink. The lids looked swollen and heavy. And her skin was burning.

Mary had a fever. A high one.

The child began to shiver, and Madelyn put her arm around her to try to keep her warm. Matthew crossed to the other side so Mary could lie down with her head in Madelyn's lap, and he seemed about to fall asleep against Mark's shoulder. Mark gave Madelyn a reassuring glance.

Melanie regarded Madelyn with a look that fairly shouted that all of this was her fault.

"I think it would be wise to stop early for the night," Robert said in a deliberately casual voice. Obviously, he did not want to alarm the younger children. "It will mean an extra day on the road, but I do not like the look of this heavy snow."

"Yes, Robert," Madelyn said, matching his tone. "I should be happy to stop soon."

Unfortunately, though, they had parted from the main road some time ago, and there had not been a village or an inn within their sight for miles. Furthermore, Madelyn began to fear they were lost. At last they saw light shining from candles in every window of a small cottage up the hill.

Robert stopped to inquire at the cottage about the proximity of an inn, but he returned to say they must not be far from his estate because the old woman inside, a Mrs. Gibbons, was his former nurse who had retired some time ago to keep house for her son. Her son had since died, but she continued to live in his house alone. Mrs. Gibbons insisted that Robert bring them all in at once to stay the night, for this was not fit weather for a family to be gadding about in. She was eager to meet his wards again, for she had not seen them since she left the Langtrys' employ and they were babies visiting with their parents.

"Here, Mary, love," Robert said, holding out his arms for the child. She stirred listlessly from the half-doze she had fallen into and went to him at once. He held her in his arms like a baby, and he looked down at her with concern when she sighed and nestled her cheek against his shoulder.

"So cold," Mary murmured. Her teeth were chattering.

"I know, sweetheart," he said. "I know."

He looked up at his eldest nephew, who got down from the coach next.

"You'll help the others, Mark?" he asked.

Without waiting for a reply, he turned and carried his niece into the cottage.

"Thank you, Mark," Madelyn said as he handed her down. She gave the tiny, primitive-looking cottage a dubious look.

Melanie hunched her shoulder and jumped down unassisted when her brother would have taken her hand.

"Come along, Matt, old fellow," Mark said cheerfully as he poked his half-dozing brother.

"Go away," Matthew muttered irritably, screwing his eyes shut and batting at Mark with one chubby hand.

"He's always like this when he's been asleep," Mark said for Madelyn's benefit. "Grouchy as an old *bear!*"

On the final word, he reached in to extract his brother and ducked the boy's attempt to push him away with flailing arms.

"Get down, Matt. Don't be a baby," Mark admonished him.

These words worked like magic, and Matthew grudgingly obeyed. Even so, he and Mark cuffed each other all the way into the cottage.

Madelyn preceded them inside and stood on the threshold for a moment to blink in the sudden glare of several lamps and candles.

"If it would not inconvenience you overmuch, Lady Madelyn," Melanie said peevishly, "we would like to come in out of the cold, too."

"I beg your pardon," Madelyn said as she quickly moved all the way inside to give them access. She thought it was a good thing for Melanie that Robert had not heard her address Madelyn in that tone of voice.

When her eyes adjusted to the smoky interior of the cottage, Madelyn perceived that Mary was now lying on one of two small beds at one end of the cottage and a very old woman was bent over her. Robert was busying himself in making up the fire in the fireplace.

"Poor little mite," the old woman crooned. "Don't fret, child. You'll be better as soon as you have some of my special cordial."

Madelyn quickly moved to the woman's side.

"Mary?" she said, touching the child's forehead.

"Mama," the little girl said, looking up at her. "I knew you would come."

Madelyn was horrified. The fever obviously had disordered her mind!

"No, Mary. I am not your—" She broke off with a shocked look at the old woman.

She had *pinched* her!

Madelyn bit her lip, conscious that Robert had

looked up in alarm from where he was tending the fire.

"I'm right here, darling," Madelyn said, touching Mary's hot little face. The old woman gave her a nod of approval.

"Don't go away again," Mary said, whimpering.

"No, my dear," Madelyn said solemnly as she met and held Robert's gaze. "I won't."

"Good," the old woman whispered. "Maybe she will sleep now."

Madelyn nodded and held Mary's hand as tears threatened to spill down her face. If something happened to Mary, she would never forgive herself.

"You will be here when I wake up?" Mary asked.

"I will be here," Madelyn said. "I promise."

Mary made a little mewling sound like that of a lost kitten and closed her feverish eyes. Her face smoothed out.

Then she was still.

"Is she—" Madelyn began in panic.

"Only asleep," the old woman said. "You can see the rise and fall of her chest."

Mrs. Gibbons straightened with a hand at the small of her back for support.

"You did well," she told Madelyn. "So, you're the society lady who broke my Robin's heart. Well, you're pretty enough to make the boy lose his head, and no mistake."

Madelyn stared at her with incomprehension and wondered if she was wandering in her wits.

"Mrs. Gibbons," Robert said in an injured tone. "You *promised*."

"I remember well how you mooned over Lady Madelyn that last year I was with your household," the old woman cackled.

She favored Madelyn with a speculative look.

"Will you have him, after all, your ladyship?" she asked, her eyes bright with interest.

"Mrs. Gibbons," Robert said in despair, but the corners of his mouth quirked up. The situation was *so* ridiculous.

"You could do *much* worse. He's a good boy," Mrs. Gibbons went on, "except for a bit of a mischievous streak, but I wouldn't give you a brass farthing for a man without a bit of the devil in him. Robin had the sweetest heart of all my charges."

"I'll keep it in mind," Madelyn said dryly.

The old woman laughed as if Madelyn had made a vastly amusing witticism.

"Well, we had best decide how we are going to sleep," Robert said, obviously eager to change the subject. "Are there more blankets, Mrs. Gibbons?"

"Aye, and quilts, too, young master," she said expansively. "There isn't much to do these days to keep a body active but make 'em and put 'em away in the hope they'll be useful someday. You or the little boy can have my bed, and the rest of us will have to lie down by the fire."

"Nonsense! We cannot put you out of your own bed!" Robert exclaimed.

Then he broke off and gave Madelyn a conscience-stricken look.

"Lady Madelyn, forgive me, I did not think—"

"I agree completely that Mrs. Gibbons should sleep in her own bed."

"Lady Madelyn will sleep in the chair near the child, of course," the former nurse said in a voice that brooked no argument. "She promised to be with her when she awakened."

"Of course," Madelyn said after a short silence. In her heart, she was panicked. What if she said the wrong thing to Mary when she awakened? What if she *did* the wrong thing? She had never had the responsibility for a child before, and she felt completely inadequate to deal with the situation.

What if the girl took a turn for the worse and Madelyn, in her ignorance, did not recognize it for what it was?

She knew from Robert's and Mrs. Gibbons's grave expressions that Mary's condition was serious. If the worst happened—if the child did not survive—Madelyn would never forgive herself.

She had prided herself on her many accomplishments, but she knew now that all of her expensively acquired skills were shallow and useless. Playing the pianoforte. Embroidering linen handkerchiefs with scores of different, intricate stitches. Singing arias in flawless French, German, and Italian.

What good were they to her—or anyone—now?

She had difficulty *dressing* herself without help, for heaven's sake!

"I shall be perfectly comfortable in the chair with a blanket or two," she said in a voice that brooked no argument.

Robert gave her a look brimful of gratitude, but Madelyn looked away from him.

She didn't deserve it. The wooden, straight-backed chair was a more pleasant alternative to the floor of hard-packed earth, after all.

Satisfied that Mary would sleep undisturbed for the time being, Mrs. Gibbons and Madelyn arranged a nest of blankets around the fire for Robert and the children to sleep upon.

To her embarrassment, Madelyn had never tried to do such a thing in her life and had no idea how to go about the business. Mrs. Gibbons quietly instructed her as Melanie gave her a look of utter contempt at her helplessness.

Then she went back to the chair drawn up by Mary's bed and sat down to keep watch over the fitfully sleeping child.

"You will call me if there is any change?" Robert said quietly sometime later as he placed a quilt over her. Madelyn started, for she was so exhausted that she had fallen into a light doze.

Some angel of mercy *she* was going to be, she thought with self-loathing. In sudden panic, she realized that she wouldn't recognize a "change" if she saw one!

However, she strongly suspected that what was needed now was a show of confidence, and not only for the child's sake. Robert looked as if all the burdens of the world had been placed on his shoulders.

"Of course, *Robin*," she said with an attempt at humor.

He smiled wanly at her.

Then he went next to the fire and sat with a blanket around him, staring into the darkness of the shadowed room as if keeping watch over the huddled bodies of his sleeping wards.

Ten

Mary opened her eyes and looked around her in alarm, but then she gave a big sigh of relief.

Her head hurt, her eyes stung, and her throat burned like fire, but *she* was here. Mary could hardly see her in the darkness, but she could feel her hand lying on her chest.

Whenever her children were sick, Mama slept in a chair beside the bed and rested her hand lightly on the child's chest to reassure herself that her baby was still breathing. She couldn't sleep herself otherwise, she insisted. It always made Mary feel warm and safe no matter how sick she was.

Mary yawned, and Mama came awake with a start.

"It *is* you," Mary said, pleased as she bent her head to kiss the soft hand that cupped her cheek. Mama didn't smell as lovely as usual, but that was all right.

"Go back to sleep, Mary," her mother whispered. "You will need your rest if you are to get better."

"My throat hurts."

"I know, love. I'm sorry."

Mama was whispering, probably because she didn't want to wake up Papa, Melanie, Mark, and Matthew.

"I'm thirsty," Mary whimpered. Papa didn't like it when she whined like a baby, but her body ached all over.

"Here, drink this," Mama said, raising Mary's head so she could drink from a cold earthenware mug. Her throat hurt even more when the cold water went down, but she felt better, anyway. Her body was like a desert, craving comfort.

"You won't go away again?" Mary asked anxiously as she peered into Mama's face. She could only see the shape of her in the darkness.

"No, I won't go away. I'll be here as long as you need me."

Reassured, Mary smiled and lay back with a breath so deep it made her chest hurt a little. She was so hot she tried to kick the blanket off, but Mama kept it firmly in place with her hand.

Mary wasn't in her own bed, she knew. And she vaguely remembered that long ago someone told her Mama was dead and in heaven with the angels.

Maybe in heaven the angels let your Mama come home if her children were sick.

Or maybe Mary was dead, too, and *this* was heaven.

If so, that was all right as long as Mama was with her.

Madelyn smoothed Mary's matted hair back from her hot forehead as she slept.

"How is she?" Robert asked anxiously as he bent over the bed beside her.

"She woke up and asked for water. That is a good sign, surely?" Madelyn asked hopefully.

"Yes. The best," he said, sounding relieved as he put his hand on the child's forehead. "She is still feverish, but not, I think, as hot as she was when we put her to bed. Did she seem to know you?"

"I think she did," Madelyn said cheering slightly. "She asked if I was going away again, so she must have remembered that I stayed with those other women at the inn. I am so sorry I didn't stay with you. I had no idea Mary would—"

Robert cupped Madelyn's cheek with a gentle hand. Madelyn was suddenly aware of the fact that her clothing was rumpled, her hair was a rat's nest, and she had not bathed for days. She wondered that he could bear to touch her. She could not look him in the eye for embarrassment.

"Madelyn, my dear, it is not your fault Mary is ill," he said so tenderly that she wanted to weep with gratitude. "This happens with children. Fortunately, they are rather hardy little creatures for the most part."

He was pretending confidence to reassure her, for the slight quaver in his voice gave him away.

For a long time he stood behind Madelyn with his hands on her shoulders as they kept vigil over Mary.

Mary woke up once and looked straight up to see the two shadowed figures bent over her, but since the smoke from the lamp hurt her eyes, she closed them again.

Everything will be all right, she mused, reassured, as sleep overtook her again.

Mama and Papa were both with her.

Dawn was peeking through the windows when Madelyn woke up and wriggled to give some relief to her cramped limbs. When she did, she looked down to see that Robert was braced in a sitting position on the floor next to her chair, sound asleep, his head resting halfway in her lap. She couldn't resist stroking his dark hair.

She smiled, then touched Mary's forehead.

"Robert!" she exclaimed with a start, finding Mary bathed in sweat. "Robert, wake up!"

He was at her side bending over Mary's bed at once.

"I think the fever has broken," she whispered, for Mary was still asleep.

"Thank God," Robert said fervently. "Thank *you*," he added, kissing Madelyn full on the lips in his relief.

When he realized what he had done, he drew back as if scorched.

"I did nothing," Madelyn said, looking away in embarrassment.

Hearing the commotion, Mrs. Gibbons joined them at the child's bedside. Madelyn had been vaguely aware of her checking on Mary at intervals throughout the night.

Mary woke up and stared at the three pairs of eyes surrounding her.

"Mary, sweetheart," Robert said. His voice broke a little. "How do you feel?"

"I'm all wet," Mary complained, looking anxious.

"It's all right, dearie," Mrs. Gibbons said soothingly. "We will change your clothes in a trice. Lady Madelyn, you may get her out of her wet things while I find her something to wear."

Madelyn looked after her in surprise as she bustled off, and she then started extracting the sick child from the nest of blankets. Robert brought over the ewer of water.

Matthew sat up and stared stonily ahead with red-rimmed eyes.

"Is Mary dead?" he asked, his lips trembling. Mark patted the boy on the shoulder and whispered to him.

The bodies of dead people, Madelyn realized with a shock, were brought home, washed, and clothed. She wondered how exposed these poor children had been to the rituals of death when their parents' corpses had been brought to the house years ago, after the fatal carriage accident.

Robert went over to Matthew and sat down to draw him into his lap. Mark, although he would have scorned to let his emotion show, sat close beside them.

"No, Matt," Robert said. "She's better today. We think she will be all right."

The little boy's face was transformed with relief. Melanie inched toward her uncle as if she would seek comfort as well, but at the last minute she stopped and looked straight at Madelyn.

Madelyn was not fooled by the girl's appearance of unconcern. There were dried tears on her cheeks.

Her heart wept for these poor children.

"Melanie, I could use your help to turn her over," Madelyn said on impulse.

Melanie gave her a wan smile and rushed to help her.

"It was you sitting with me last night, wasn't it, Lady Madelyn?" Mary asked as Madelyn dried her damp body with a towel.

"Of course, my dear," Madelyn said, smiling at her. "Who else would it be?"

"No one, I guess," Mary said solemnly.

Eleven

It was the day before Christmas Eve, and Lady Madelyn and the Langtrys were still enjoying Mrs. Gibbons's hospitality.

Mary, though her condition was greatly improved in the past few days, was still too fragile to undergo the daylong journey to her home. It would be unwise in the extreme, both Mrs. Gibbons and Robert insisted, to cut her convalescence short.

Besides, Mrs. Gibbons was quite alone in the world, since her son died some months ago. The snow had fallen off and on in the days since her unexpected guests had arrived, and Robert did not have the heart to leave her behind to spend Christmas alone. It was obvious that she rather enjoyed having company.

Food was no problem for the time being. Mrs. Gibbons had plenty of dried apples and oats for porridge.

Robert and Mark had taken her son's guns and gone hunting to bring home a half-dozen rabbits that Mrs. Gibbons cooked to perfection with some savory herbs. Then they were fortunate enough to kill a deer, so there would be venison for Christmas dinner.

How could Robert disappoint them all by insisting that they go home?

Robert split another log with Mrs. Gibbons's late son's ax and continued to rehearse his arguments for staying at the isolated cottage a while longer, even though he was perfectly aware of the truth.

He wanted to stay because after they went home to Yorkshire, Madelyn would continue on her journey to her cousin's house and he might never see her again. The house party at Lord Blakely's estate was an unusual circumstance; he and Lady Madelyn hardly moved in the same social circles.

As if his mind had conjured her, Lady Madelyn walked out of the cottage to join him.

He had to smile.

The ravishing slave to fashion that was Lady Madelyn had undergone an amazing transformation.

She was still dressed in the same clothes she had worn when she left Lord Blakely's estate, and they had not withstood their adventure well. She had combed her hair straight back and secured it with a piece of ribbon in a vain attempt at neatness. Springy curls had escaped along her temples.

Then she smiled at him, and he thought her— still—the most beautiful girl in the world.

He had thought he was in love with her years ago, but he had been mistaken.

Then he had been in love with her beautiful face and her lively intelligence. Now he had seen a glimpse of her soul.

No one could have nursed Mary more tenderly than this society lady. She had willingly, if a bit ineptly, helped Mrs. Gibbons prepare meals, and she set the table with mistletoe and holly and pine boughs she gleaned from the woods with Matthew's enthusiastic assistance.

She had been kind to Matthew and Mark; she had been patient with Melanie.

With Robert she had been everything that was proper.

He sighed.

She probably could not wait to get back to civilization, and he was deliberately holding her back.

"I wondered where you had got to," she said cheerfully.

"I've got to earn our keep," he said, feasting his eyes on her smile.

The snow had stopped, and the land was blanketed once again with a pristine, unblemished blanket that sparkled in the sunlight. The air was as crisp as an autumn apple.

"Mary is chafing to go outside," Madelyn said, getting to the point of her errand, "and Mrs. Gibbons thinks that a bit of fresh air will do wonders for her spirits if we bundle her up very warmly."

"And what do *you* think?" Robert asked.

"What do *I* think?" she repeated in disbelief. Apparently it never occurred to her that anyone would ask her opinion.

"You have spent as much time nursing Mary as any of us. Do you think she is well enough to come outside for some fresh air?"

"Yes," she said, giving him a smile that transformed her face. "I think if she has to stay in the cottage much longer, she will fret herself into a relapse. There is nothing so good for the lungs as fresh air."

"That settles it, then," Robert said easily, putting down the ax and picking up an armload of wood.

Eyes wide with panic, Madelyn blocked his path.

"You are going to let *me* decide?" she asked, shocked. "No, Robert. It is too much responsibility! I know nothing about children!"

"My dear, you seem to have a special rapport with

this particular child. I am certain your judgment can be trusted in this."

He walked around her and proceeded to the cottage, but she soon overtook him and sped through the doorway ahead of him to gather all the blankets she could find.

Madelyn wondered if this was what it felt like to be part of a family.

Mrs. Gibbons declined to join them on their outdoor adventure because she was cooking stew, so the excursion included just the Langtrys and Madelyn.

Mary was enshrouded in blankets and enjoyed all the attention of her brothers, sister, and uncle, who kept tucking the blankets up against her face to protect her nose and ears, petting her and hugging her. When they walked in the woods to enjoy the hushed loveliness of a new snowfall in the white-dusted trees, Madelyn thought that this, at last, was the peace she had sought all her life.

The sky was so blue. The air was so clean and pure. And the snow sparkled like crystal in the sun.

Robert carried Mary in his strong arms, but the little girl insisted on holding Madelyn's hand in hers as Madelyn walked beside Robert. Matthew, instead of chattering like a squirrel for once, was looking about him with bright, curious eyes.

Melanie stalked ahead with a big stick in her hand as if she were an Amazon warrior escorting a party of travelers through enemy territory. Her hair had been tamed to the semblance of order by a determined Madelyn, an indignity to which Melanie ordinarily would not have submitted. The danger to her sister had left Melanie on good behavior, for her.

Madelyn noticed, not for the first time, that

Melanie possessed a barbaric sort of beauty that would be quite striking when she matured into her strong features. Even so, she knew better than to imply as much to Melanie. The girl had made it clear that she neither sought nor welcomed Madelyn's approval, even though it was plain that the girl's less than conventionally pretty appearance bothered her. Madelyn could have told her that good looks were not only far overrated in terms of one's happiness but also that they were largely a result of careful grooming and expert tailoring rather than an indiscriminate blessing bestowed by the Almighty.

Madelyn gasped when the party entered a smooth clearing ringed by crystal-frosted oaks. Birds nestled in the branches and serenaded the bright, clear morning.

"Here we rest, poppet," Robert said, giving Mary a squeeze before he lowered himself to a fallen log so that she was perched on his lap. "You are heavier than you look."

Madelyn was shocked that Robert would make such an uncivil remark to any female, regardless of age, but Mary merely giggled.

She would never understand children. Never.

"I wish we could stay here forever," Mary blurted out, reaching for Madelyn's hand when she sat down next to Robert.

Robert made a show of feeling her forehead.

"Darling, I think the fever is coming back. We must take you back to the cottage without delay and have Mrs. Gibbons pour some of her nasty black concoction down your throat!"

"No!" Mary said in alarm. Although Mary was a relatively good patient, she had made it clear that she did not appreciate her hostess's attempt at nursing her with folk remedies. "Lady Madelyn, after we leave here, you will come and see us sometimes, won't you?"

Madelyn looked into those clear blue eyes still touched with pain, and lied.

"Of course I will, darling," she said around the lump in her throat.

When she returned to her old life, she would be deluged with responsibilities. She had spent too long on the Continent nursing her broken heart, but she found she couldn't run away from love.

Unfortunately, she had found that Robert obviously didn't lose a night's sleep over her. He had not been suffering alone all this time, as Madelyn had. He had been nurturing his surrogate family, as well he should.

He didn't need her at all.

None of them did, really.

Mary was only clinging to her because she reminded her of her mother for some obscure reason, and she had been ill and in need of comfort. Matthew was friendly enough, but he was amiable to anyone who would pay attention to him. Madelyn didn't flatter herself that Mary and Matthew felt any special affection for her that couldn't easily be transferred to a more suitable woman of Robert's choice.

Mark was polite enough, but he was practically on the verge of adulthood. Any woman in the household would do well enough for him.

Melanie would never accept her.

And Robert would never accept a wife who was not acceptable to all his wards. He had made that perfectly clear long ago.

But she pushed all of this into the back of her mind. She had a few days to enjoy Robert and his family before she returned to her old, lonely life, and she would enjoy them.

"Mary, love," Robert said to the little girl. "I think it would be all right for you to walk about a bit if Melanie and Mark will hold your hands and shield you from the wind."

Mary gave him a beatific smile at the prospect of exercise, and Robert extracted her from her cocoon of blankets to put her on the snow-covered ground. Melanie took her sister's hand and carefully put her arm around her shoulders as if she were a little old lady she was afraid might break. Mary grinned and took off at a smart trot as Melanie squeaked with surprise.

Madelyn and Robert laughed heartily, but Madelyn looked away when she realized that they had been smiling with quite shocking intimacy into one another's eyes. She felt his fingertips on her chin and then his lips as he gave her a fleeting kiss. The sweetness of it brought tears to her eyes.

She swallowed and walked away for a short distance to give herself time to recover. Mark, Melanie, and Matthew ran around the clearing and threw snowballs at one another. Madelyn noticed that although Mary threw snowballs at her brothers and sister, no one threw them back at her.

"Mary!" Robert called. "You must not become overexcited, love. You are to walk calmly or we will have to go back inside."

His voice sounded perfectly normal, Madelyn thought in dismay. Kissing her meant *nothing* to him. Just a diversion for a winter afternoon, quickly forgotten.

She was dimly aware that the children had ceased their running and shrieking. Mark and Melanie flanked Mary to keep her in order, and Matthew walked backwards in front of her to keep her amused.

Madelyn had to smile.

How she would miss them, even Melanie. For all her prepubescent surliness, the girl had a good heart. She could tell this by the way she talked softly to her sister and clung tightly to her hand as if she were afraid someone might take the little girl away from her. She might be jealous of Mary's prettiness and adorable ways, but she loved her.

Madelyn slowly walked back to Robert, who was watching her with a questioning look in his eyes. Her heart turned over when he offered her a sprig of mistletoe he apparently had picked while she was watching the children. Hesitating slightly, she reached out for it. He took her hands and drew her down beside him.

Absurdly, he placed the mistletoe in her hair.

She must look ridiculous.

Before the thought was finished, he kissed her softly again.

"We should take Mary back before it gets too late," he whispered.

It is already too late, Madelyn thought in despair.

Melanie felt the old panic rise as she watched Uncle Robert and that Lady Madelyn. Her uncle probably thought no one saw him kiss her, but he was mistaken. Melanie had not taken her eyes off them for a minute.

Of course he was impressed by her precious ladyship's devotion to Mary in her illness, but Melanie was not fooled.

It was easy to be an angel of mercy when the sick child is pretty and adorable.

If Melanie had been the one to become ill, Lady Madelyn would have left her out in the cold to die.

Quite deliberately, Melanie stooped and packed some snow into a hard, icy ball regardless of the fact that she had forgotten her gloves and the frozen stuff felt as if it were burning her unprotected hands. In her present mood, she welcomed the pain.

Then she let the missile fly and watched with grim satisfaction as it struck Lady Madelyn squarely between the shoulder blades.

After that, it all came in slow motion.

Lady Madelyn's shriek of pain.

Her brothers' and little sister's cries of dismay.

They were looking at Melanie as if she were a stranger.

"How *could* you?" Uncle Robert asked, giving her a heartbreaking look of disappointment.

Matthew and Mark stepped away from Melanie as if they were afraid of being contaminated by her touch.

Tears filled Melanie's eyes as she watched Uncle Robert put an arm around Lady Madelyn's shoulders and tenderly touch her face in comfort as if she were the most precious thing in the world.

Melanie had lashed out with all the anger and frustration and hurt in her troubled soul to put an end to the idyllic little interlude between her uncle and that woman.

Well, she had succeeded.

Only now Madelyn was in Uncle Robert's arms and Melanie was the outsider.

It was strangely quiet that evening as Robert, Mary, Matthew, and Mark huddled around the fire for warmth and ignored Melanie completely except for a reproachful glance now and then.

Melanie and Lady Madelyn stood apart. Lady

Madelyn was talking to Mrs. Gibbons, probably because she couldn't stand to look at Melanie's face, Melanie thought as she tried to stop the tears pooling at the corners of her eyes from falling.

Melanie would not apologize. She would *not!*

Robert had demanded that she beg Lady Madelyn's pardon at once, but in response Melanie had only given Lady Madelyn's back a killing look.

"Do you think her royal highness cares what any of *us* think of her?" Melanie sneered.

"Just because Lady Madelyn is rich and the daughter of an earl does not mean she has no feelings," Robert said vehemently. "I would not have her suffer such insult at the hands of one of my family for anything in the world. You are quite old enough to know the difference between kindness and cruelty, and what you did was *cruel.*"

"She didn't mean it," Mark offered timidly. "We were all throwing them."

"It was deliberate," Uncle Robert insisted, giving Mark a look that discouraged him from further ill-advised attempts at mediation. "It was rude and malicious. Melanie *did* mean it, and she *will* apologize. Not because I require it but because it is the right thing to do."

"Melanie?" Mary called plaintively. "You didn't mean it, did you? You wouldn't hurt Lady Madelyn on purpose."

She would. She *did*. And her uncle knew it. The lump in Melanie's throat grew so big she could hardly swallow.

"Melanie," Uncle Robert said in such a gentle tone of voice that the tears spilled over at last. "Be the sweet child I know you are. Apologize."

"She despises me, and I don't blame her." Melanie

whispered. "I hate myself. I wish I were dead instead of Mama."

Uncle Robert had given her a look of such compassion that Melanie couldn't stop her shoulders from shaking with her suppressed sobs. She would give anything she possessed at that moment if her uncle would give her a hug and tell her everything was going to be all right.

"Lady Madelyn does not despise you," he said instead, giving her that sad, sad look. "You have only to apologize and she will forgive you."

He sounded so sure. Like all men, he thought Lady Madelyn's heart was as pure as her beauty. Even now, after days of living in a dirt-floored hut with no clean clothes and no maid to arrange her hair, she was beautiful.

"Lady Madelyn," Uncle Robert said, raising his voice. His eyes remained on Melanie. "My niece has something she wishes to say to you."

Lady Madelyn turned around and looked at Melanie, just as if she hadn't heard every word that had been said between them. She walked to the other side of the room and beckoned Melanie.

It was cold so far away from the fire. It almost felt good to Melanie.

She *deserved* to be cold.

"I . . . should not have thrown the snowball," she whispered haltingly, bracing herself for Lady Madelyn's anger. "I am . . . sorry."

This was the lady's opportunity to tell Melanie just what a miserable little worm she was, and Melanie had no doubt she would take advantage of it.

Instead, she laughed. Actually *laughed!*

Lady Madelyn's laugh was high and musical, like her singing.

"You are forgiven, of course," Lady Madelyn replied graciously. "I understand your motives completely."

"You could not possibly understand," Melanie said stiffly, certain that Lady Madelyn was laughing at her.

"Oh, could I not?" she asked with one raised eyebrow. "Did you not know that my father was a famous general and diplomat and after my mother died I was his hostess?"

"Grandmother said so," Melanie said uncertainly, wondering what *that* was to the purpose.

"My mother died when I was sixteen," Madelyn said with a sigh. "After that, I hosted my father's parties and received a great deal of attention thereby. My father was very rich and very handsome and very successful as a diplomat. All the best people came to our parties. If my father had remarried, I would have been forced into the background again. I was not about to tolerate that."

A mischievous smile played at her lips.

"My good girl," Lady Madelyn said, patting Melanie on the head. "When it comes to ridding oneself of undesirable competition, no one can hold a candle to *me!*"

"You mean . . . *you*—?"

"Oh, certainly! I hope you do not think you are the only person in existence who is afraid that if her father—or uncle, in this case—takes a bride, he will cease to love his children."

"What did you do?" Melanie asked.

Lady Madelyn put a companionable arm around Melanie and leaned close. After a moment's whispered conversation, Melanie burst into a peal of laughter.

"You *didn't!*" she breathed. "I never thought of putting sugar in someone's shoes so the insects and mice would nest in them."

"Compared to me you are the veriest amateur."

"Did your father ever find out?"

"Of course! She went to him immediately and laid the whole before him. She told him that she could never marry a man who had engendered a wicked girl like me."

"Did your father punish you?"

"I was far too old for that. Besides, he never did believe I was capable of such a diabolical act. He was sad for a long time, because he did miss her. But in the end I persuaded him that she only wanted him for his money and the privilege of being his hostess. A woman who really loved him would have managed to tolerate his little beast of a daughter, after all."

Lady Madelyn looked sad.

"I chased them all away, and in the end he died a lonely man," she said with a sigh. "He never did have the sons he wanted so badly to inherit his title. I told myself I would someday marry and give him grandsons and that would be just as good. Unfortunately, he died before I could do so, and I cannot begin to convey to you how much I regret that."

Lady Madelyn gave Melanie a bright smile and a little pat on the shoulder.

"Now we will tell your uncle that it is made up between us, and you can be comfortable again," she said, turning to the little group by the fireplace.

Comfortable.

Melanie doubted she would ever be comfortable again.

Twelve

Madelyn was fascinated by Mrs. Gibbons's and the Langtry children's excitement over Christmas.

In Madelyn's world, Christmas was hardly a memorable occasion. The opening of the Season, for example, was anticipated with far more pleasure. She had spent more than one Christmas alone except for servants and thought nothing of it.

Today, however, she found herself drawn into the preparations for the Christmas feast, even though she had vowed not to set foot near Mrs. Gibbons's scrubbed worktable since the day she found the elder woman cheerfully dismembering rabbit carcasses for the pot.

Madelyn had known that food underwent a great deal of transformation before it was presented at table, but the sight of the tiny rounded backs so suggestive of those possessed by human infants made her stomach give an alarming lurch. It was only by exerting the strongest willpower that she was able to consume a single morsel.

In like manner, the sight of the gutted deer hanging from a tree outside preparatory to Robert and Mrs. Gibbons's cheerful butchering had struck her with absolute horror at such barbarism. She tried to keep Matthew from seeing it, only to overhear him asking Robert with bloodthirsty glee if he could take the head home to scare Amy and Aggie Whittaker with the next time they came to visit their relatives in Yorkshire.

He, like Robert and Mark, seemed to think that shooting an innocent forest creature was a masculine act of valor deserving of extravagant feminine praise, which Mrs. Gibbons, Mary, and Melanie were happy to supply. Madelyn couldn't bear to look at the pathetic thing hanging by its back legs. She was strongly reminded of a cat's posturing when it presents its mistress with a dead mouse.

Wisely, Mrs. Gibbons whisked the raw cut of venison she was preparing for the fireplace spit out of sight before she invited Madelyn and the children to decorate sweet biscuits with a sugar icing she had improvised from the contents of her larder. It amazed Madelyn that she could produce biscuits without a proper oven.

Soon Madelyn and Mary were laughing as she helped the child draw wobbly little wreaths, with the aid of rolled-up paper, like a pastry chef. Madelyn had seen the technique in Paris and been fascinated. On her own estate, however, it would never occur to Madelyn to throw her servants into confusion by invading her own kitchens to try her skill.

"Let me try! Let me do it!" cried Matthew, wiggling all over like a puppy in his eagerness to decorate the biscuits.

"You just want to get close enough to eat them," Melanie said accusingly as she patted her brother on the head.

Madelyn lifted Mary down from the table and helped Matthew hop up unassisted. His painstakingly executed wreath was wobbly, but he only grinned and bit into the confection when the other children laughed at it.

"No fair eating your mistakes, Matthew," Madelyn chided him playfully. "Now you will do another, and try to hold your hand steady. There, you see? That one was much better." She anticipated his intention of devouring the biscuit by removing it from his reach. "None of that, young man!"

He grinned, unrepentant, and licked the untidy remains of the previous biscuit from his lips.

Madelyn and Melanie reached for the spoon in the bowl at the same time, and their hands touched. For a moment they smiled into one another's eyes with laughter-filled faces. Then, embarrassed, they looked away.

A blast of cold air from the direction of the cottage door heralded the arrival of Robert and Mark, who had been chopping wood.

Even though the wind was cold, Robert had been working in his shirtsleeves with the cuffs rolled up to bare his strong forearms. A heart-melting smile burst across his face as he caught Madelyn helping the children decorate biscuits.

"How delicious!" he said when he came up behind Madelyn. His voice was so husky that Madelyn imagined for a moment that he must be talking about her rather than the confections she and the children were making.

That, of course, was highly unlikely considering the deterioration her appearance had undergone since their residence at the cottage. Her once-presentable traveling clothes were crushed and getting soiled about the hem. It was true that she had several clean gowns in the trunk salvaged from the accident, but she couldn't bring herself to put any of her lovely evening ensembles on over her unclean body. She had not changed her underpinnings since she left Lord Blakely's estate. Besides, the gowns' fabrics were so delicate and the necklines so low that she would freeze to death!

And her hair . . . Madelyn did not like to think about the horror she had experienced when she looked at her face in Mrs. Gibbons's only mirror. There wasn't much even she could do with tresses that were dank from almost a week of utter neglect. She had taken to combing her hair straight back and braiding it around her head. This Quakerish coiffure probably made her look as if she were forty, but it was the best she could do.

Foolishly, Madelyn scraped the spoon on the side of the icing bowl and blushed crimson in embarrassment at being discovered by Robert in so domestic an occupation. She was accustomed to being adept at everything she put her hand to, and being the merest amateur at any activity was disconcerting.

She was probably doing it all wrong. Mrs. Gibbons patiently had corrected her several times as she tried to be useful.

The sound of Mary and Melanie giggling alerted her to the fact that Robert and Mark had each snatched a biscuit.

"Save those for the feast," Mrs. Gibbons called out from where she was turning the venison on the fireplace spit.

The meat was still oozing bloody juices, and Madelyn turned quickly away. Once again, she regretted her ineptness in being too squeamish to help her with such matters.

Madelyn could recite the various kinds and quantities of spices required by any chef to produce the dishes that a noble household would expect to see at table, and she knew down to the last handkerchief how much the household linens should cost and where they are to be procured, but her knowledge was theoretical rather than practical.

She looked up at Robert in time to watch him savor the last of his purloined biscuit.

"Delicious," he repeated softly as he looked into her eyes.

Not one of Count Andreas Briccetti's elaborate compliments had made Madelyn blush, but she felt her face grow hot.

Robert turned to the others, breaking the spell. Madelyn wasn't sure whether she was relieved or disappointed.

"I have a proposal to make," he said, raising his voice. "Traditionally, the men go out to bring the Yule log into the house, but I propose we all go. For one thing, Mark and I have cut quite a *large* log, and we may need help to carry it."

"Me, too?" asked Mary hopefully.

"You, too," Robert said, touching the top of her head as he looked down at her.

"Robert, do you think that would be wise—" Madelyn began in concern.

Mrs. Gibbons pursed her lips in disapproval.

"The night air kills," the old woman said gravely. "You'd best stay in tonight, child, and let the men bring in the log."

"We will bundle her up quite carefully," Robert said, unwilling to disappoint the child. "She is nearly well."

Even so, Madelyn could see that Robert was already having misgivings. He looked from Mrs. Gibbons's reproachful face to his niece's triumphant one. How like a man to blurt out his proposal before he had completely thought through the consequences!

"*Men,*" muttered Mrs. Gibbons, for once ignoring

the distinction in rank between herself and her former nursling.

Madelyn very much wanted to join Robert on the torchlight procession to retrieve the Yule log, but like Mrs. Gibbons, she questioned the wisdom of allowing Mary to embark upon such an adventure. It was one thing to allow her to enjoy the bright winter sunlight for a quarter of an hour. It was quite another to send her into the cold dark of night.

"I will stay behind with Mrs. Gibbons," Madelyn said casually. "There must be *some* witness to the magnificent spectacle you will present from the window as your torches recede into the woods."

She glanced casually at the smallest girl.

"Perhaps you would like to stay with us, Mary," she said. "We can have the table ready and sample the biscuits to make sure they are good enough for the rest of them."

Mary hesitated, torn between the adventure and staying indoors with all of Madelyn's attention directed to herself.

Mrs. Gibbons opened her mouth, apparently to join her word with Madelyn's, but firmly snapped her lips shut when Robert gave her a significant look. He must have realized, as did Madelyn, that any attempt to influence Mary would harden her intention of accompanying the group to fetch the Yule log.

"I will stay with you," Mary said, trustfully putting her small hand in Madelyn's.

Robert gave Madelyn a look brimful of gratitude, and Madelyn smiled at him.

"It isn't proper for women to bring in the Yule log. It could mean bad luck for all of us," Mrs. Gibbons muttered.

Madelyn could see Melanie's hackles rise in anticipation of Mrs. Gibbons's objection to *her* going with

Robert and her brothers, but Mrs. Gibbons wisely refrained. Melanie was as healthy as a horse, although she probably would not appreciate the comparison, and there was no reason on earth why she shouldn't join the males in retrieving the log. Unless Madelyn missed her guess, the girl's back was strong enough to make a real contribution.

That evening, Madelyn and Mary, who was standing at Madelyn's side wrapped in a blanket from neck to ankle, watched from the doorway as the procession of log-bearers wound their way into the forest. The little girl was hopping on one foot and then the other with excitement.

"It is just like when I was little and Grandfather, Papa, and Uncle Robert used to bring the Yule log home," she said, her eyes sparkling up at Madelyn when the flickering torchlight had moved out of sight and Madelyn closed the door.

Madelyn felt the now-familiar lump harden in her throat. These children had been robbed of so much in their young lives.

And a younger Madelyn had wanted to rob them of still more by advising Robert to send them all off to boarding schools. How arrogant she had been, so confident in her own judgment and in her power over Robert.

"Will you come home with us and marry Uncle Robert?" Mary asked innocently. "You *like* Uncle Robert, do you not, Lady Madelyn?"

Madelyn stared down at the child's earnest face.

"I like your uncle very much, but—" she began carefully.

"Oh, *please* say yes, Lady Madelyn! I know he wants to marry you, for he told me so."

"He *did?*" Madelyn said, disgusted with herself for feeling giddy as a young girl upon being presented with a nosegay of flowers by her first beau. "Are you certain he was not funning you?"

"Oh, no," Mary said seriously. "Uncle Robert would never joke about being in love. It is too important."

"When did he tell you this?" Madelyn couldn't stop herself from asking.

"This morning, when you went out to the pump with Melanie to fetch water for Mrs. Gibbons. I asked him if he would marry you so you could be with us always, and he said he would like nothing better. Only he said you were much too fine for us and you would soon go back to your big house and your many servants and forget all about us."

Mary paused and looked searchingly into Madelyn's face.

"You will not forget us, will you, Lady Madelyn?" she asked anxiously.

"No, darling," Madelyn said as the tears formed in her eyes. She was turning into *such* a watering pot all of a sudden. "I will never forget you."

Satisfied, Mary gave Madelyn a hug and chattered happily with Mrs. Gibbons as she fussed over the meat on the fireplace spit and the single cake she had made from the best of the dried apples in her root cellar. The child kept running to the window, adorably trailing blankets, to see if the others were returning yet.

Madelyn arranged the table with Mrs. Gibbons's best plates and bits of mistletoe and greenery she had gleaned from the forest.

It was the only contribution to the feast she was qualified to make, she thought sourly.

She was much too fine for them, Robert had told Mary.

He couldn't be more wrong.

He and these marvelous children were much too fine for *her.*

"They're coming, they're coming!" Mary cried out, hopping up and down in her excitement. Madelyn peered into the night and felt her own heart lift the way women's hearts must have lifted for generations at the sight of their men hauling in the huge logs for their Yuletide hearths. The men welcomed a chance to flex their muscles before an admiring audience, and women welcomed the promise of warmth and the hope of prosperity for the coming year.

Madelyn felt a primitive thrill as Robert came in first, carrying one end of the log, with Mark and Melanie between them struggling with the other part. Matthew's participation was mostly honorary, for he was too short to do more than walk alongside with his hand on the log as he struggled to make his short legs keep up with his elders. This did not stop him from puffing his chest out with pride as the waiting ladies applauded their efforts.

Miraculously, the log *just* fit in the fireplace, and everyone's voices were hushed as Robert, as honorary patriarch, lit it with a splinter of wood saved from the previous year's log. When the flames took hold, everybody cheered.

"Now, a toast!" he said as Mrs. Gibbons distributed small clay goblets of her best homemade wine to all, even the children.

"To our friends," he said, looking straight at Madelyn before he turned to nod to Mrs. Gibbons. "May they have good health, long life, and great happiness."

Madelyn felt tears sting her eyelids again, this time with affection as her eyes locked with Robert's.

"Come, now," Mrs. Gibbons said prosaically. "Let us sit down before the food gets cold!"

The children cheered and quickly took their places at the table. There would be no more toasts; only laughter and the satisfying sound of a family thoroughly enjoying plentiful food and lovingly prepared sweets.

Madelyn could not remember when she had enjoyed a meal more. She blushed with pleasure when everyone praised the little cakes she painstakingly had decorated. They were nothing special, really. Any of her highly paid chefs would have raised their eyebrows in scorn at the sight of the lumpy treats abundantly decorated with more of Mrs. Gibbons's icing. But one would think they were the most elaborate concoctions produced by the most famous of Parisian artists from the enthusiastic way they were appreciated by Robert's family.

Suddenly ravenous, Madelyn was appalled to realize she was devouring the venison so enthusiastically that juices were running down her chin. She furtively looked around to see if anyone had been watching her unladylike display.

Robert had, of course, and he smiled at her with warmth and amusement. Madelyn grinned apologetically and tucked back into the delicious meal with a gusto that would have left any of her strict teachers utterly speechless.

There was more homemade wine after dinner, and Robert made a point of telling Mrs. Gibbons that he would send her wine from his own cellar to make up for the inroads they had made into her carefully preserved hoard.

This thought sobered Madelyn immediately.

Once Christmas was over, they would return to their old lives. Mary was nearly well, and there was no reason why Madelyn could not resume her journey to her cousin's house. Robert would have business at his estate and his own people to look after.

The children would once again become involved with their lessons.

They would forget all about her.

When the last of the wine had been drunk and the children were nodding off with weariness, Madelyn felt Robert's hand on her shoulder and looked up to see him bending over the back of her chair to speak to her.

"Time to go to sleep, Madelyn," he said. "We must present a united front on this or the children will try to stay up all night."

"I could not blame them," Madelyn said wistfully. "I do not want the night to end, either."

Robert's answer was a convulsive grip on her shoulder. Madelyn was so sleepy that she couldn't be sure, but she thought she felt a fleeting touch that might have been his lips on the top of her head.

"Well, I am exhausted," she said, standing up and yawning conspicuously. "Come along, sprite," she said to Mary, who had already opened her mouth to object. "You don't have to go to sleep yet. We'll just lie down by the fire and watch the others for a while."

To Madelyn's surprise and gratification, the little girl obeyed her. Once Mary had recovered, she had joined the group sleeping in front of the fireplace. Robert had cut soft boughs of pine and improvised pallets cushioned with blankets for them so they would not have to sleep directly on the dirt floor. Madelyn had grown to like the way their hair and clothes smelled of fresh greenery.

This night, as she dozed off, she was surprised to find Melanie as well as Mary curled by her side.

Melanie looked as surprised as Madelyn felt.

"There's a draft," she said, looking a little embarrassed.

Madelyn merely smiled and gathered both girls close.

So this was what it was like to have children in one's life, she thought as she dozed off.

Robert's heart turned over when he picked his way to his own pine-bough pallet and saw Madelyn sleeping in a nest of little Langtrys. Not long after the girls bedded down, Matthew had gone to join them, curling up like a puppy at Madelyn's feet.

With a smile gently curving her full, lush lips, she looked like an angel.

How could anyone dismiss this beautiful, generous woman as an empty-headed society ornament? Even his mother would have been forced to eat her words about Lady Madelyn's shallowness if she had been with them.

The earl's daughter had exerted herself with good humor and good intentions to help take care of the children. It was plain that she had never undertaken such labors in her life, but she made up for her lack of experience with single-minded determination. Not once had she expected anyone to take care of *her*.

Her once-soft and pampered hands were raw from fetching water and washing in the strong lye soap Mrs. Gibbons made each spring. She had shared what must seem to her the most austere hardships without complaint.

If only—but Robert couldn't allow himself to think about that.

Lady Madelyn was not for him. She had never been for him.

Once they left this place, she probably would not think or speak of them again unless it was to fashion a droll story about her ghastly experiences in the wilderness for the amusement of her fashionable friends.

She was his for one more night, he told himself, refusing to give into maudlin regrets.

With that, he removed his coat and moved in close to Melanie so they were all sleeping together.

Thirteen

"Pardon me, Madelyn," Robert said nervously, "but isn't that a sapphire necklace my niece is wearing?"

Madelyn gave him an unconcerned smile. He noticed that she had adorned her disreputable-looking traveling clothes with a magnificent set of emeralds that set off her auburn hair and green eyes delightfully. With an unerring eye for fashion, she withdrew an intricately patterned cashmere wrap from the trunk and placed it around her shoulders even though the cottage was warmer than usual. The Yule log, carefully tended by Mark and Robert, had blazed throughout the night, for it would have been bad luck to let it go out.

"One is never too young to appreciate fine jewels," Madelyn said with a fond smile at the proud little girl. "See? It even makes her stand taller."

She held aloft something that flashed red fire on her palm.

"Come here, Melanie," she called to the other girl, who was watching Mary enviously. Melanie gave her a hopeful look and came to stand obediently before her. "Rubies for you. Remember that when you have a husband. Rubies, perhaps relieved with diamonds or emeralds occasionally, and don't let him try to tell you that mere garnets will do just as well because they are the same color. They're not."

Melanie gave her a brilliant smile as Madelyn pinned a pretty brooch at her shoulder and placed two ruby-and-diamond clips in her slightly oily hair. Then she scampered off to show the rubies to Mary.

Robert flinched. If either girl had a mishap with Madelyn's gems, it would take him years to make restitution.

Much as he hesitated to spoil their pleasure, he felt he had to object.

"Madelyn, I don't think it's a good idea to lend your jewelry to these little hoydens," Robert said, watching Madelyn with a sense of foreboding as she sat in a chair by the fire with her jewel case before her. Obviously her jewels had been packed with her evening gowns.

"Nonsense. It's just for one day," Madelyn said, smiling. "We must do honor to the feast, don't you agree?"

He had to smile back.

It was Christmas Day, the sun was shining, and he was with the people he loved best in the world except for his mother, but she was not precisely in his best books at the moment, anyway.

Mrs. Gibbons had sentimental tears in her eyes.

"Last year I celebrated Christmas with my son, who was hale and hearty then. I never thought I'd bury him before a year had passed. I expected this would be the saddest Christmas of my life." She sniffed and forced herself to smile. "But here are all of you, come to cheer me in my loneliness. God is good. When I was a child, my parents always burned candles in the windows at Christmastime to guide the Christ Child to our door, and this year the candles guided you to me."

"You are such a darling, Mrs. Gibbons," Madelyn said, giving the old lady a hug. "Only a saint would be thankful to Providence for foisting six uninvited guests on her!"

"Being with the children makes me feel young again," she said wistfully.

"I think you need a bit of sparkle, too," Madelyn said, poised over the contents of the jewel box. "Mary may look lovely in sapphires, and Melanie shall be famous for her rubies when she takes London by storm, but you, my dear Mrs. Gibbons, must have diamonds."

"Oh, Lady Madelyn, I *couldn't!*" Mrs. Gibbons objected, her eyes sparkling, when Madelyn pinned a diamond brooch on the front of her plain apron.

But Madelyn merely smiled as Mrs. Gibbons reverently touched the glittering gems.

"I've never worn such a thing in all my life," she said, awed.

They sat down to slightly plainer food than last night—stew, bread, the broken remains of the little cakes. But it tasted like ambrosia.

The children sang Christmas carols, and Madelyn even showed them all the steps to a dance she had learned last autumn in Paris.

It ended all too soon.

In the blink of an eye, it was time for the girls to relinquish the borrowed gems to Madelyn so she could lock them in the little velvet-lined casket. All of them helped Mrs. Gibbons wash the dishes in her homemade lye soap and put them away.

After the children and Mrs. Gibbons had gone to sleep, Robert walked to where Madelyn was sitting pensively by the fire and kissed her forehead. His heart was full of gratitude for the way she had made his wards happy today.

The touch of her skin against his lips made him draw back in alarm to peer into her face.

She was burning up.

"Madelyn?" he said questioningly.

She smiled wanly at him.

"You are ill! Why did you not tell us?" he exclaimed.

Robert put a hand to her cheek, hoping that he had been mistaken, but she was unmistakably feverish. He had attributed her high color and occasional sneezing to smoke from the Yule log. Now he knew why she had grown quieter as the day progressed and why she kept gravitating to the fireplace.

"It was such a beautiful day. I did not want to spoil it," she croaked. Robert could have wept for the loss of her beautiful voice. No wonder she had insisted upon leaving most of the singing to the children. How could he not have noticed? "Besides, Mrs. Gibbons would have insisted upon dosing me with that vile concoction of hers, and that would have soured the taste of our delicious Christmas feast."

Stew. Hard little rounds of bread baked days ago in the fireplace ashes. Robert doubted that Madelyn had eaten such poor fare in her entire life. His heart filled with remorse.

"But what am I to do with you?" he asked, feeling helpless.

She placed a hot hand against the side of his cheek, and he turned to kiss it.

"Nothing," she said. "I shall rest now and be much better in the morning."

She rose, then, and Robert drew the folds of her cashmere shawl closer to her throat. She had been clinging to the thing all day for warmth, he knew now, rather than vanity.

Instead of bedding down in her usual place between the girls, she set herself apart, apparently to keep from spreading the contagion to him or one of the other children.

"You will be cold there," he said.

"I will be cold anywhere," she croaked with a glimmer of grim humor. "Good Lord, I sound like a frog."

"Never," he whispered as he piled his share of the blankets on top of her. She didn't object, which told him how wretched she must feel.

During the night he checked on her several times, but then he accidentally woke Mrs. Gibbons, and she insisted upon taking over the nursing duty.

"Poor lady," Mrs. Gibbons said sympathetically as she washed Madelyn's hot face with a cool cloth.

It seemed Robert's prayers were answered and they were not going to have to leave tomorrow, after all. But at what a price!

Madelyn was so much worse the next morning that Mrs. Gibbons insisted that she lie down upon her late son's bed, most recently occupied by Mary, and stay there all day. And her condition did not improve during the following week. New Year's Day found her miserable.

"I will be all right, sweetheart," Madelyn croaked when a concerned Mary bent over her with tears in her eyes.

"Drink this, your ladyship, and don't waste your breath arguing," said Mrs. Gibbons as she purposefully bore down on Madelyn with her dark, smelly brew.

Madelyn stoically closed her red-rimmed eyes and obeyed, which set her into a fit of coughing and shivering. She then got up and went to sit in the chair by the fire, which now resembled a throne because the younger children had cushioned it for her with what seemed like the entire contents of Mrs. Gibbons's linen chest.

How sweet they are, Madelyn thought, succumbing to sentimental tears. How could she bear to leave them?

Melanie carefully arranged the cashmere shawl around her shoulders. Madelyn started to thank her, but she ended up coughing instead.

"My poor dear," Robert whispered. "How in the world am I to get you to your cousin's house now?"

"I will be ready to leave by tomorrow as planned," Madelyn said resolutely. "You gave me a week to recover, and I have had it."

"Absolutely not! You are much too ill to travel."

"I shall manage. We cannot in good conscience impose on poor Mrs. Gibbons any longer," Madelyn said.

He nodded, for he knew she was right. They *had* to leave. His horses had consumed most of the hay and oats upon which Mrs. Gibbons's mule and cow should have been able to subsist until spring. He, Madelyn, and the children had eaten her winter provisions, and they had to go back if for no other reason than to arrange for Mrs. Gibbons to receive food, hay, and grain to replenish what her uninvited guests had consumed.

It was time for the idyll to end.

And it did, much sooner than anyone had anticipated.

Madelyn, who was dozing in the chair after another sleepless night, awoke with a cry of alarm when an imperious knocking sounded at the door of the cottage. When it was not answered immediately, a crash resounded from the other side as if someone were attempting to bash the door in.

Matthew, Mary, and Melanie were wide-eyed with fright. Madelyn stood on weak knees and stepped in front of them with the vague thought of protecting them from intruders. Mark picked up a poker, ready to defend them all, if necessary. Robert shook his head at the youth, and he sheepishly put it down.

Then Robert squared his shoulders and opened the door, forestalling Mrs. Gibbons when she would have done so. After a terse, low-voiced conversation with whoever was outside, Robert stood back and admitted several burly men.

Unbelievably, they were wearing the livery of Madelyn's own servants. Her now-recovered guard, the muscle-bound giant John, peered into the cottage, and his mouth gaped open when he saw Madelyn.

Foolishly, she reached up to tidy her hair and colored in embarrassment.

"It's all right," Madelyn said soothingly to the children, who were frightened by the arrival of these big, menacing-looking intruders. She faced John and scowled at him. "You are frightening the children," she snapped.

"I beg pardon, my lady," he said, meek as a lamb.

"Darling," Madelyn's middle-aged cousin, Elizabeth, exclaimed as she ran into the cottage and all but crushed Madelyn in her arms. Madelyn winced. Every bone in her body ached. "At last we have found you. We have been searching for days. We had almost lost hope when John recognized Mr. Langtry's carriage in front of this cottage."

Madelyn stood back and looked at her cousin. Her mind was perfectly blank.

"Oh, my poor dear! What can have happened to you?" Elizabeth looked ready to weep. "When we received your letter and you did not arrive last week, we suspected the worst!"

The middle-aged woman gave Robert a look that made him color hotly.

Mr. Kenniston, heavily favoring his right leg with his cane as he entered the cottage, peered inside and ostentatiously waved his hand in front of his face to dispel the smoke from the fireplace.

"Madelyn!" he exclaimed, utterly appalled by her appearance. "Good God!"

His eyes narrowed as he glared at Robert.

"You!" he said, pointing at him with his cane. "What have you to say for yourself?"

Robert faced Madelyn's irascible guardian bravely. She could imagine how he felt at being confronted by the man who had refused his suit for Madelyn's hand twice and, if Madelyn knew Mr. Kenniston, in less than tactful terms.

"*Look* at her!" The older man spat with a gesture that encompassed the dirt floor, the smoldering fire, and Madelyn's bedraggled appearance. "She looks *ill*, and it could not happen at a worse time!"

"Mr. Kenniston, none of this is Mr. Langtry's fault," Madelyn began, finding it strange to refer so formally to Robert.

"Have you found her?" a cultured, slightly accented voice said from the doorway.

Madelyn stared, certain that the fever must have made her delirious, for there, standing in Mrs. Gibbons's humble cottage, was a familiar golden-haired man with piercing blue eyes dressed in such exquisite clothes that he might have been on his way to an embassy reception.

"*Carissima,*" he said, his voice soft with so much compassion that tears of self-pity sprang to Madelyn's eyes. He took both her hands in his.

He looked so beautiful and smelled so good. Madelyn felt utterly humiliated to have him see her like this.

"Come, my sweet. We have come to take you home," he said gently.

"Are you a prince?" Mary asked, her eyes taking in the magnificence of his splendid black coat and his immaculate white linen.

He smiled. He had a soft spot for children and had told Madelyn he hoped to have many after he found a suitable bride. She remembered that quite clearly about him. It was one of the many reasons, aside from his wealth and title, that Lady Letitia had insisted he would make the perfect husband.

"No, little one," he said to Mary, obviously pleased by the implied compliment. "Permit me to introduce myself. I am Andreas, Count Briccetti, at your service."

He bowed to the dazzled little girl as if she were a princess, and she solemnly curtsied the way Madelyn had taught her.

"Do not worry, my dear," Elizabeth said tearfully as she took Madelyn's arm and tried to step between her and Mary. "We will take care of you now."

Mary burst into tears and clutched Madelyn's leg. Melanie put her arms around Matthew to stop him from following. He turned around and buried his face in his sister's neck.

Madelyn pulled herself out of Elizabeth's sweetly scented embrace and touched the top of Mary's head. Robert quietly stepped forward and led the little girl away to stand with his hands on her shoulders as if to prevent her from further interference.

"But we've been so worried," Elizabeth said, looking hurt. She probably had expected Madelyn to express *some* joy at seeing her would-be deliverers.

"When you did not arrive as expected, we immediately made inquiries and found there had been an accident to your coach. Your maid arrived without you. Then Mr. Langtry's coachman drove up to the house in your carriage with your coachman and guard. No one knew what had happened to you, Madelyn, but Mr. Kenniston, upon learning that Mr. Langtry had stopped to give aid to the passengers, immediately suspected—"

She broke off and blushed furiously.

"That is—" she stammered, "he thought—"

That he had abducted you for your money. Or worse.

"Never mind," Madelyn said hastily. Of course, that is exactly what her former guardian and companion would think if the earl's daughter was missing. "As you can see, I am quite well."

"So I can see!" Elizabeth exclaimed sarcastically. "And here is Count Briccetti, come to pay his respects."

Madelyn gave the count a dumbfounded look. Her brain really was *not* working. The last time she saw him was during a ball at his palace in Venice. Why would he come all the way to England to call on her, unless . . .

"We shall speak of it later," he said softly as he caressed her cheek.

She may be feverish. She may be confused. But there was no mistaking the look in the man's eyes. He had come to England to pay his addresses to her! A look at Mr. Kenniston confirmed her suspicion. No wonder the poor old man was so alarmed by the sad deterioration of Madelyn's appearance. Here the most eligible suitor on the Continent had come up to scratch and she looked a perfect fright!

Unbelievably, the count did not seem in the least

taken aback by her slovenliness. His manners always had been flawless.

"Oh, my lady!" cried Bettina, practically flying in the door to run to her mistress. "Your hair!" she mourned, absolutely shocked. "And your poor *hands!* What have you been *doing* to them?"

"Nothing that cannot be rectified," Madelyn said, finding herself using the same tone with which she comforted the children as she hastily thrust her red and roughened hands behind her. "As you can see, I am quite well," she repeated. She broke off with a cough.

"We must get you home," Elizabeth said solicitously, "and into a hot bath and warm bed at once!"

A hot bath.

A warm bed.

Madelyn's eyes filled with tears at the mere thought of clouds and clouds of hot, fragrant soapy water. To make her humiliation complete, her nose started running.

Count Briccetti withdrew his handkerchief with a flourish and held it tenderly to her sore nose as if she were a helpless child.

Then he swept her up into his arms and walked to the door. Mrs. Gibbons bobbed a curtsy and opened it for him.

"Wait!" Madelyn croaked as the cold air slapped her in the face and made her nose burn like fire. "I did not say good-bye to the children."

"They will understand, *carissima*," he said, obviously intending to ignore her objections.

She found it nearly impossible to resist.

A hot bath.

A warm bed.

She was so ill and so weary.

"No!" she cried, finding the strength to push

against the count's strong shoulders until he had no choice but to put her down. She turned and glared at her would-be saviors.

"How *dare* you just barge into Mrs. Gibbons's home and insult these kind people who have taken care of me all this time? But for them, I would have been stranded. I should like to say good-bye to the children properly, *if* you please!"

Count Briccetti, looking absolutely stunned, bowed.

"I beg your forgiveness," he said without a particle of sarcasm in his voice. "We will not leave until you are ready, of course."

Her guardian, her cousin, and her maid were all looking chastened, and Madelyn realized that she had hurt their feelings.

She forced a smile to her lips.

"I thank you all for rushing to my rescue," she said, trying to sound grateful. "I know you meant it for the best."

"Oh, my lady!" her maid blurted out. "If anything had happened to you, what would have become of us all?"

Elizabeth gave the girl an impatient scowl and would have snapped a reprimand at her for forgetting her place, but Madelyn put up a hand, and her cousin fell silent.

Madelyn realized that, like Robert, she was responsible for the souls who had been placed in her care. No wonder they were so horrified by her disappearance. If she died, her estates, which employed hundreds of people, would be turned over to the crown in the absence of heirs and sold to the highest bidder. She had neglected all of the caretakers for her birthright much too long.

"Please, Madelyn. We must get you home at

once," Mr. Kenniston said wearily. Now that the excitement was almost over, he looked like the frail old man he was.

Madelyn could tell that Elizabeth was holding her breath as she approached Madelyn again. No doubt she would order a hot bath for her as soon as they arrived at the little house in Yorkshire.

Once again, the seductive vision of clouds and clouds of scented lather in a tub of hot water by the fire made her knees weak with longing.

Even so, when she looked at Mary's devastated little face, she almost told them all to turn around, go home, and mind their own business.

"Did your family come to take you home, Lady Madelyn?" the child asked wistfully.

Her family.

Madelyn started to correct the child; then she realized that with her usual perception Mary was right.

Madelyn had been lamenting the fact that she had no family, but in truth, *these* were her family, and they had been frightened half to death for her. While the dependents on her estate would be at the mercy of whoever bought Madelyn's various properties in the event of her death, Mr. Kenniston and Elizabeth would be more than adequately provided for in Madelyn's will, and Mr. Kenniston, at least, knew that. It wasn't just duty that had sent them out into the cold of winter in a desperate quest to find her.

It could be nothing but love.

Madelyn sank to her knees so that she and Mary would be on the same level.

"Yes, my dear," she said softly, wiping a tear from Mary's sweet face. "I must go with them now, but—" She broke off.

But what?

"But I will write to you," she finished lamely.

"And visit us sometimes?" Melanie asked. "Please?"

Madelyn felt a smile burst over her face.

"Yes, darling. Of course I will," she said, touching Melanie's dark head with real affection.

She shook hands with Matthew, Mark, and Robert. It seemed so inadequate. With tears welling in her eyes, she thanked Mrs. Gibbons for her hospitality.

Then, with their usual efficiency, her dependents gathered her up and swept her out to the coach. John shouldered Madelyn's heavy trunk, and the remaining footmen followed in a protective phalanx as if they feared Robert might attempt to stop them.

Madelyn felt a hysterical gurgle of laughter bubble to her lips when she saw the way Elizabeth, Bettina, and Mr. Kenniston crowded together on the forward seat of the coach, leaving her to sit with the count. All of them looked as if they were trying not to inhale, and Madelyn could hardly blame them. She must reek to high heaven.

She allowed the tears to run down her cheeks at last, and she lifted Count Briccetti's sweet-smelling handkerchief to her eyes.

"There, there, my dear," Elizabeth said soothingly. "You will be home soon and can forget this whole unfortunate experience."

She is gone, Robert thought idiotically.
Just like that, she is gone.

The girls and Matthew were in tears, and Robert firmly dragged his mind away from his own loss to comfort them.

"Lady Madelyn has her own house and her own responsibilities, just as we have ours," he told them. "It is time we went home, too."

Home.

Robert shook himself from his numbed stupor. He had to be strong for the others.

"Mrs. Gibbons, will you come with us?" he asked. The proud old woman hesitated.

"We could use your help in the nursery," he added.

Mrs. Gibbons smiled.

"I'd enjoy being useful again," she admitted. "And I've grown fond of the children."

"There, then. It's settled," Robert said, forcing himself to smile.

His life would go on, even though a piece of his heart would always be missing.

Yesterday, before reality intruded, he had resolved to ask her to marry him just as soon as she recovered from her illness. When she was with him and the children, he dared to hope that they could find happiness together.

Now all was at an end.

How could he have been so stupid?

For all that she became sentimental in a little cottage at Christmastime and entertained the children with charm and sweetness, he could hardly expect her to dedicate her life to them as he had vowed to do after his brother's death.

He had been wrong to hope.

Thank heavens the world had intruded before he had forced that kind and gallant lady into the awkward position of refusing him.

She would marry Count Briccetti, of course, and like a storybook princess, she would live happily ever after.

Fourteen

Madelyn sat at the mirror and watched Bettina put the finishing touches on an elaborate coiffure adorned with hothouse gardenias.

Was this ice queen *her?*

She seemed a stranger.

Her dress was of white crystal-beaded lace; diamonds sparkled at her throat and earlobes. Her hands were covered in long white kid gloves, and she wondered what her fellow revelers at her birthday ball would think if they could see her still-reddened knuckles. Not all the sweet-smelling lotions from the best shops in London had been effective in returning her hands to their former soft and pampered smoothness, and Madelyn was secretly glad.

Tonight's ball would be a formal notice to society that she had attained her majority and was now her own mistress. Mr. Kenniston, meticulously fulfilling the term of his guardianship, had summoned all the managers of her estates during the past few weeks to wait upon the heiress and swear the modern equivalent of an oath of fealty. As soon as the last cough and wheeze subsided, she toured the estates with these managers and gave them their orders for maintaining the properties and managing the many souls that cared for them. Then she visited London to be fitted for new gowns to replace those that had been lost in the carriage accident and to meet with her bankers.

Madelyn was not just a woman possessed of a handsome fortune, she realized at last. In effect, the fortune possessed her.

An ice queen.

That's what her reflection in the mirror showed her.

Even so, she often woke in the night with the scent of pine in her nostrils and Robert's face in her mind.

It had been almost a month since she had been removed from the cozy little cottage by her well-meaning dependents, and for the week she lingered in Yorkshire recuperating from her illness, she had clung to the hope that he would come to her. She missed Robert and the children abominably.

She had heard nothing from him, though. Nothing at all.

Not a visit. Not a letter. Not even a message.

"Thank you, Bettina. That will do," she said, feeling weary all of a sudden.

Another ball.

She would assume her social mask and fulfill her responsibilities to the souls who depended on her.

Count Briccetti had been tender and kind. He had begged her in terms eloquent enough to steal any woman's heart to marry him. Mr. Kenniston was jubilant. Here, at last, was a match worthy of the earl's daughter.

Lady Letitia, when she visited Madelyn briefly in London, had been ecstatic. She couldn't wait to tell all of their acquaintances about Madelyn's brilliant conquest.

"How fortunate it is that you had the good sense to refuse Mr. Wyndham," she gushed, as if Mr. Wyndham had not rejected *her* to marry his Pamela.

"Once you are married to Count Briccetti, you will spend part of the year in Venice, of course, entertaining at the palace. My darling child, the moment I saw you and the count dancing together at the Carnival ball, I knew it was *meant!*"

The count, careful of her reputation, stayed at an inn during her convalescence in Yorkshire and brought her armloads of hothouse flowers practically every day. Madelyn learned that although he had been filled with ardor at the very first sight of her, propriety forbade him to speak until he had first obtained her guardian's permission.

The fellow feels just as he ought, Mr. Kenniston had said approvingly, which was his highest praise for a gentleman who had not served His Majesty's government as either a diplomat or a military officer and was a foreigner besides. Mr. Kenniston had no patience with the newfangled notion that a hopeful young man should make his intentions known to his lady *before* he applies to her guardian for his consent.

While Mr. Kenniston and Elizabeth were amazed that Madelyn had not yet given the count an answer, the gentleman himself was the soul of patience.

But then, neither the count nor anyone else seriously considered that she might not agree to marry him.

Elizabeth had let it slip that everyone was expecting an "interesting announcement" that evening. What could be more romantic than for Madelyn to accept the count's proposal at the ball? The announcement would be made at midnight.

"You sly girl," Elizabeth had said coyly when Madelyn demurred, not believing for an instant that Madelyn did not mean to have him.

Madelyn barely restrained herself from rolling her eyes in frustration.

Instead, she pasted a smile on her face.

Surrounded by well-wishers, she would not let anyone guess that her heart was broken.

What right had *she* to be unhappy, after all?

"Lady Madelyn, you grow more radiant every time I see you," Count Briccetti said, bowing low before her as if she were a princess of royal blood.

She favored him with a polite smile and inclined her head before she accepted his hand for the dance. It was midnight, and she felt as if she had a fine film of sand covering her eyelids. Thank heaven it was almost time to go into supper.

A swarm of prospective suitors had descended upon her at the beginning of this dance, each hoping to escort her into the supper room. The count had vanquished them all with one aristocratic look, which just proved that everyone considered her as good as his.

Madelyn was in no mood to listen to his polished flattery, but she paid him the compliment of looking directly at him instead of letting her eyes wander in search of someone more interesting.

This was not mere courtesy; she knew that the only man she wanted to see would not appear in her ballroom this night.

When the dance was over, she accepted the count's arm into the supper room and stood smiling graciously from her place at the head table as all the fine ladies and gentlemen raised their crystal glasses of French champagne to her.

After all, it was not *their* fault she would infinitely

prefer a portion of homemade wine served in a common clay mug with earthy sediment in the bottom.

The children had fallen asleep in the coach, but they came to life when Robert gave an exclamation of relief at seeing the lights of the manor come into sight. There was a candle in every window, and Robert was reminded nostalgically of Mrs. Gibbons's little cottage and her eagerness to welcome the Christ Child and any stranded travelers the spirit of Christmas might send her.

He hoped with all his heart that Lady Madelyn would be as glad to see him and the children; otherwise, he would feel like a complete idiot.

Steady on, old fellow, Robert told himself bracingly.

"Are we at Lady Madelyn's house yet?" Melanie asked, sounding cranky.

"Yes, darling," Robert answered as the coach swept into a long, winding lane to the house. What if Madelyn wasn't here? It seemed to the anxious Robert that they had spent a year rather than two weeks on the road following Madelyn's trail from one to another of her holdings. For a lady who had appeared to be at death's door a month ago, she had covered an amazing amount of territory.

Robert had wasted two precious weeks nursing his broken heart when the children came to him in committee and asked why he had not gone after Madelyn to beg her to marry him.

It had been plain to the simplest mind that he was grieving.

"Can you not tell her how much we miss her?" Matthew asked. "If you don't, she might marry that prince instead."

"He's a count, stupid, not a prince," Melanie scoffed.

"It isn't that simple, Matt," Robert said, giving Melanie a look of reproof for being unkind to her brother. "Lady Madelyn *should* marry Count Briccetti. He would be more suitable for her. Marrying me will ruin her life."

"Grandmother says Mrs. Crowley is unsuitable for Mr. Wyndham," Mary asked innocently. "Does that mean she has ruined his life? He seemed very happy when they called upon us."

Robert sighed. How like his mother to say something like that in front of the children! As did every woman of her generation, she saw marriage only as a way for a young lady to obtain security and social standing and for a man of position to obtain a handsome dowry and a wife with the proper bloodlines to father his heir. Mr. Wyndham's father had not approved of the match, and it remained to be seen if he would disinherit his heir because he defied him by marrying Pamela, anyway.

Pamela and her girls had been blooming after the simple wedding at the parish church, and Mr. Wyndham himself seemed thoroughly contented with his new family. The way he looked at his bride made it clear that he did not regret his choice for a moment.

"No, dear," Robert said patiently. "Mrs. Crowley did not ruin Mr. Wyndham's life by marrying him because she—"

He broke off and stood up a little straighter.

"Because she loves him," he said slowly as comprehension dawned. "And he loves her."

Hang suitability! Madelyn would care *nothing* for the wealth and prestige marrying Count Briccetti could give her, so why should Robert give it a passing thought? That fellow could never make her happy,

for he couldn't possibly, in a million years, love her
as much as Robert did!

If Madelyn had been born of merely respectable
parents and Robert had been the one with the title
and handsome fortune, would he have hesitated to
marry her?

No. Not for a moment.

Robert's qualms about proposing to Madelyn had
nothing to do with the fact that she might not be
happy with him as a husband or that she could not
adjust to living with his wards. Their time together
in Mrs. Gibbons's cottage effectively dispelled that
notion.

No. Robert's stubborn refusal to ask the woman
he adored to marry him had everything to do with
his own injured pride in not being able to provide
more for his wife than she would bring to him.

True, Madelyn had not renewed her expressions
of everlasting regard for him, but he could hardly
blame her for that. In his pride and superior male
arrogance, he had been quick to dismiss her words
when she told him repeatedly two years ago that she
did not give the snap of her fingers for her fortune
or the *haute tôn*'s approval.

It all seemed very silly now.

"You are absolutely right, Matt," Robert said,
aware that the children were regarding him with
hopeful looks on their faces. "I shall leave at once!"

Robert felt guilty for dragging the poor little
things all over the country in search of Madelyn, but
they had insisted on coming.

Melanie, speaking for them all, was quite determined to be present when he proposed to Madelyn
for fear he would botch the job. Secretly, he was relieved. Much as he deplored his niece's lack of faith

in his powers of address, he was enough of a coward to want the advantage of the children's support.

In truth, if Madelyn accepted, she would be marrying them as well.

He encountered the first line of resistance at the door.

"I am afraid Lady Madelyn is entertaining guests this evening," the haughty butler said, looking down his nose at Robert.

Robert knew he must look unkempt and rather wild-eyed. He had been on the road for so long that his jaw was starting to bristle with whiskers and his clothing, although donned fresh that morning, was in sad condition. The children were sleepy-eyed and cranky. Mark was propping up the two youngest to keep them from falling asleep on their feet.

"If you would be kind enough to convey my card to Lady Madelyn—"

"I am afraid that is impossible," the butler said.

"I am certain she will see us if—"

"On no account can I disturb Lady Madelyn this evening," the butler said slowly and clearly, as if to a simpleton.

"It's *cold*," Mary whimpered. "Why will you not let us come inside?"

Robert looked down at her perplexed little face and felt the rage grow in him.

He was weary, hungry, and missing Madelyn like mad. The children had been traveling for days. If the officious butler wanted to call in all the footmen to thrash him, Robert was of a mind to take them on!

With a determined scowl on his face, he prepared to shove his way into the doorway.

"Very well," the butler conceded grudgingly, "you

may wait in the back parlor. You will not disturb anyone there."

"And you will take my visiting card to her at once?" Robert persisted.

The butler glanced down at the card. His eyes widened, and he gave Robert a penetrating look.

"Have I grown three heads?" Robert asked politely.

"I will inform Mr. Kenniston that you have arrived," he said, regaining his icy composure. "If you and your . . . companions will follow me, Mr. Langtry?"

Mr. Kenniston, Robert thought with a sigh. He could imagine the reception he would receive from *that* disapproving gentleman.

At that moment, Mary decided to take matters into her own hands. Quick as lightning, she ran around the butler and shot through a door being held by a startled footman. Before the man could shut it to prevent further invasions, Matthew followed his sister, nearly knocking the footman down.

Mark gave a whoop, and he and Melanie followed. Robert was forgotten as the butler shouted to the footmen to give chase. Grinning, Robert shoved the butler aside and followed the footmen into the main part of the house, aware of the butler's shrill command and the pounding footsteps of hot pursuit behind him.

Lady Madelyn's guests were about to be treated to a show that would keep the gossips in transports for weeks.

Madelyn's glass of champagne dropped from her nerveless fingers and expired in a sparkling shatter of crystal and effervescence on the polished floor as

Mary skidded into the room, looked around quickly, and fixed her big blue eyes on Madelyn's face.

For a moment, Madelyn held her breath, certain she was dreaming.

Then one of the ladies screamed, and a footman ran into the room to snatch the little girl off her feet as she squirmed and kicked her feet. One of the child's slippers fell off.

Matthew arrived on the heels of the footman and gave Madelyn a big, heartwarming smile before he became distracted by the array of food on the buffet table and emerged from the platter of pastries with a chocolate éclair in each hand.

Madelyn grinned. This definitely was no dream.

"Where did those little urchins come from?" Elizabeth demanded. When the butler, looking winded, appeared in the doorway, she fixed him with a look that would cut glass. "Remove them *at once!*"

"Put the child down," Madelyn said, stifling a smile at Elizabeth's look of utter bewilderment. "Good evening, Mary. Is it not rather late for you to come calling?" She turned to greet the new arrivals. "Mark. Melanie." To her delight, Mark executed a perfect little bow, and Melanie curtsied. "How delightful to see you all, but I was rather hoping to see your uncle as well."

"He's here," Matthew said, pausing in the act of devouring a pastry. There was chocolate smeared all over his round little face. "That butler shouted to the footmen to have him thrown from the house, but Uncle Robert will draw their claret!"

"I see," she said calmly. "Won't you come sit by me, then?" She opened her arms to the children, who ran to her at once. Elizabeth gasped when Madelyn emerged from their embrace with a chocolate stain on her bodice.

Madelyn turned to a gaping footman with one raised eyebrow.

"An assortment of refreshments for my guests, if you please," she said as she settled them in the chairs her servants hastily brought forward. She gave the count a little smile of apology as he good-naturedly moved down the table to make room for the children.

"And if I find that Mr. Langtry has been damaged in any way," she added, fixing a cold stare on her butler, "I shall dismiss you without a character."

The butler pulled himself together and signaled the servants, who had been frozen in place. After a slight hesitation, they soon had set an assortment of delicacies in front of the children. Then the butler quickly exited the room, presumably to make sure Robert was still in one piece.

The count gave a long, humorous sigh as he helped Matthew to a lobster patty from his own plate.

"I must protest, *carissima,*" he said, giving her a small, regretful smile. "I can merely give you diamonds and emeralds. How can I compete with a gentleman who would give you these so charming children?"

Madelyn blinked at him in surprise, then let the words sink in. The count, with the gentlemanliness that made him a paragon among men, had just given Madelyn his blessing to find her own happiness.

"Andreas," she said, softening at the good-natured way he dedicated himself to entertaining Robert's wards. "You must be the kindest man in the world."

"That is so," he said modestly as he helped Mary cut a small fillet of tenderloin into bite-size pieces with his knife.

"Uncle Robert has come to ask you to marry him," Melanie called out to her.

"And high time," Madelyn replied, almost to herself. Tears of happiness stung her eyes.

When she would have risen to go and meet him, Andreas placed a restraining hand over hers.

"Let him come to you, *carissima,*" he said softly.

Madelyn bit her lip. He was right, of course.

Mr. Kenniston fixed Robert with a forbidding stare, and Robert could hardly blame him. By the time the butler had snapped an order for the footmen to release him, his clothes were battered, and the hat he carried in his hand was almost smashed flat.

"I must congratulate you on your clever timing, Mr. Langtry," Mr. Kenniston said contemptuously. "When you made no attempt to contact Madelyn after your carefully orchestrated little adventure in Yorkshire, I was deluded into thinking you finally had accepted your own inadequacy as a suitor for her hand. Now I realize that I was wrong to underestimate your shrewdness as a fortune hunter."

"I beg your pardon?" Robert asked, all at sea.

"Do not play the innocent with me," the old man said sternly. "The term of my guardianship ended at midnight when Madelyn officially attained the age of one-and-twenty. Now she can marry you or even the chimney sweep if she wishes without forfeiting her inheritance, and I have no legal grounds to prevent it."

"Today is Madelyn's birthday?" Robert said blankly.

"Do not insult my intelligence by pretending you did not know," Mr. Kenniston said witheringly. "I can only despise you for sending those children into the supper room to soften her heart toward a match that can only be a shocking misalliance. Have you no scruples at *all*, man?"

"I had no idea," Robert said. "I only know I cannot live without her."

"Puppy!" Mr. Kenniston snapped. "Madelyn is a highly desirable lady in both person and wealth. Do you think I have not heard the same sentiment over and over again from hopeful suitors, and in far more eloquent terms than *you* are capable of? Count Briccetti is her match in birth, wealth, and social status. What could you possibly offer her to compare with that?"

"Love. It's all I have," Robert said.

"You disgust me!" The old man spat, and turned away. "Do not prevent him," he added dryly to the footmen, who were poised uncertainly on the balls of their feet. "If Lady Madelyn is deluded enough by his mawkish posturing to accept him, it is out of our hands."

The old man's mouth had a sour twist to it.

"If you truly cared for Madelyn, you would leave now" was his parting shot.

All of Robert's old demons of insecurity crowded into his brain at the redoubtable Mr. Kenniston's words.

The footmen had magically melted away with Mr. Kenniston, and Robert was left alone in the marble-faced hall. If he went through with his intention of proposing to Madelyn tonight, all the world would agree with Mr. Kenniston that he did so only for her money.

Madelyn watched Mr. Kenniston return to the room and take his place at the table, yet no Robert had come to claim her.

Her smile faltered.

"Courage," whispered Andreas.

Madelyn walked to where Mr. Kenniston was whispering urgently to Elizabeth.

"What did you say to him?" Madelyn asked in a voice that sounded harsh to her own ears.

"The truth," Mr. Kenniston said, looking her straight in the eye. "That if he truly cared for you he would leave now."

Madelyn gave a cry of distress and looked toward the still-empty doorway.

"The fact that he apparently has taken my advice proves he is only a little less unworthy of you than I had thought," Mr. Kenniston added.

"Sit down, Madelyn," Elizabeth said softly. "Everyone is staring."

But even as she raised her head to meet the stares of her guests, she saw their eyes swivel to the doorway.

Robert stood there, his unsmiling face revealing nothing as he signaled the children to come to him.

There must have been at least a hundred pairs of eyes staring at Robert in all the dirt of his travel.

Rarely in his life had he felt so inadequate. He recognized a few faces. Lady Letitia. The Earl of Stoneham. They did not give him confidence.

"Are you going to ask her now?" Matthew asked when he had arrived at his uncle's side. "Will she come home with us right away?"

Robert smiled bleakly. If only it were that simple.

Lady Madelyn had taken a step toward him, and his eyes were dazzled by her. Her white gown shimmered with rainbow lights, and her eyes were so solemn he could have wept. She was perfect from the crown of her head to the tips of her expensively shod feet. He never had felt more unsure of his welcome in his life.

If she refused him, he would, quite simply, die.

"May I have a word with you in private, Lady Madelyn?" he asked.

"No, Robert," she said deliberately. "Whatever you have to say to me, you must say to me here."

She was not going to make it easy for him. For a moment, the seed of doubt Mr. Kenniston had planted in his mind almost triumphed.

"I will go now if that would please you," he said.

"Uncle Robert!" cried the children in near unison.

"That would not please me at all," Madelyn said. "You came here to ask me something, Robert. Do so."

"But—" he began, looking around at their now-hushed audience.

"This is who I am, Robert," she said as she indicated the room with one graceful hand. "This is *what* I am. If you want to marry me, you must ask me here, in my own house, in front of all of my friends and acquaintances. I have come into my fortune. If you offer for me now, you offer for *that* and all it entails as well."

"Lady Madelyn—"

"Ask her, Uncle Robert!" Melanie said in disgust.

He swallowed, hard.

"Lady Madelyn, will you marry me?" he asked. To his embarrassment, he heard his voice crack on the last word.

The next few moments passed with excruciating slowness as Madelyn simply looked at him. Robert felt a cold trickle of sweat drip down his back.

The room held its collective breath. Even the children were frozen in place.

Then Madelyn burst into a radiant smile and raced across the room to throw herself into his arms. Now that she was closer, Robert could see the faint smear of chocolate on her bodice, and his heart melted with love.

"Yes!" she cried between the ardent kisses she placed on his bristly jaw as Robert crushed her in his embrace. "I will marry you."

At last! At last! At last! Madelyn's heart sang as Robert twirled her around in an insane dance of happiness. He was laughing as giddily as she.

Madelyn bent and accepted kisses and hugs from Robert's delighted wards. All the sadness she had felt during those weeks of separation just melted away.

When she rose, Robert kissed her again—slowly and thoroughly this time—and she felt, as always, that she had come home after a long journey.

"A toast to our lovely Lady Madelyn," Count Briccetti's voice rang out. "May she, her fiancé, and these delightful children find great happiness in their union!"

Madelyn grinned and nodded in acknowledgment when the startled guests scrambled for their glasses of champagne and drank. She pantomimed applause and blew Count Briccetti a kiss. He acknowledged it with a demure smile and a regal inclination of his handsome head.

"Let us marry tomorrow by special license," Madelyn whispered to Robert, tucking her arm in his and anticipating with relish the pandemonium that would result.

Madelyn's serene, privileged existence was about to come to an end, and she could hardly wait!

Epilogue

London
May 1819

Of course, Robert and Madelyn did not marry the day after Robert's unconventional proposal. Robert had pointed out to Madelyn that to deny the children a proper wedding ceremony would have broken their hearts.

Now Robert wished he would have listened to her.

"She is late," Robert said to Alexander in a panic as he paced in the sacristy at St. Paul's. "Maybe she's changed her mind. Lady Letitia and her wretched cousin Elizabeth probably have been working on her since dawn."

Robert had suggested a small wedding in their parish church at Yorkshire, but Madelyn insisted that if they were going to do the thing, they would do it right—and that meant St. Paul's in London so she could show off her handsome bridegroom properly and make all of her acquaintances turn pea green with envy.

Robert had been flattered by these loverlike words at the time, but now he wished he had not given in so easily. There were at least three hundred guests in the church consulting their timepieces and whispering.

Alexander and Edward shook their heads in good-natured derision at his panic.

"Madelyn is *always* late," Alexander pointed out with maddening calm. "She can't change her mind, old fellow. She has Mary, Melanie, and your mother with her."

Even so, Robert was a bundle of nerves until Matthew came running to say that the open carriage containing all of Robert's favorite ladies, as he often called them, had pulled up in front of the church.

Robert exchanged a look of relief with Mark, who looked quite splendid in a swallow-tailed morning coat.

"It's time," Alexander said, acting as best man. He had offered to administer a medicinal shot of brandy to the nervous groom, but Robert refused it.

He had been afraid he couldn't keep it down.

But all his nervousness magically disappeared when he looked to the end of the aisle and saw Mary and Melanie, dressed in gowns of heavenly peach organza, walking toward him. They looked as pretty as the spring flowers they carried in blond straw baskets. A rainbow of blossoms crowned their upswept hair.

With them was Matthew, looking dapper in a little swallow-tailed coat that Madelyn had commissioned from the most expensive tailor in London.

Vanessa and Lydia came next in blue gowns with wreaths of flowers in their hair, and then everyone stood to face the bride.

Matthew bounced excitedly on the balls of his feet in a little-boy dance of happiness, and Robert felt like joining him.

Madelyn's exquisite gown of snowy silk embroidered with silver came straight from Paris, and the newspapers and gossips, no doubt, would describe it in ecstatic detail for days to come. But all Robert noticed was the radiant smile on his beloved's face as Mr. Kenniston escorted her to him.

The old man had at first told Madelyn he would not attend the ceremony, but when she insisted that he had stood in place of her father for years and it would ruin her happiness if he did not give her away, he capitulated.

Indeed, how could anyone resist her, Robert thought, smiling like the lovesick idiot he was.

"You seem to be in a monstrous hurry all of a sudden," Mr. Kenniston hissed sourly to Madelyn. "If you *must* marry the fellow, my girl, at least try to retain *some* dignity."

Madelyn obediently slowed her pace a bit, knowing that her former guardian needed her support to keep from stumbling without his cane.

Still, it was hard not to race ahead at the sight of her wonderful Robert and the children she adored looking at her with such expectation and joy on their faces.

"You were late," Robert whispered, kissing her hand after Mr. Kenniston relinquished her to him. "I died a thousand deaths."

"*I* knew you would come," Matthew said stoutly in a voice loud enough to make the other children snicker.

"Me, too," Mary piped up, not to be left out.

"Dearly beloved," said the clergyman in a slightly reproving tone. Even so, Madelyn could see he was struggling to keep a straight face. "We are gathered here . . ."

"It was the best wedding in the world!" Matthew declared ecstatically as he devoured meringue-covered lemon pastries at the wedding breakfast.

"I agree," said Robert, gazing into his bride's eyes. "Is it not time for you to change into your traveling dress, my love?" He lowered his voice and whispered into her ear. "I can't wait to get you all to myself."

He gave a rueful glance to where Mary and Melanie, already changed into their expensive matching traveling costumes, chatted excitedly with Amy and Aggie.

"Not that I'm likely to have you all to myself anytime soon," he said with a sigh. "Madelyn, I am delighted that you are so fond of my wards, but is it not a trifle extreme to take them along on our wedding trip?"

"Nonsense, darling," Madelyn purred. "The children will adore Paris."

BOOK YOUR PLACE ON OUR WEBSITE AND MAKE THE READING CONNECTION!

We've created a customized website just for our very special readers, where you can get the inside scoop on everything that's going on with Zebra, Pinnacle and Kensington books.

When you come online, you'll have the exciting opportunity to:

- View covers of upcoming books
- Read sample chapters
- Learn about our future publishing schedule (listed by publication month *and author*)
- Find out when your favorite authors will be visiting a city near you
- Search for and order backlist books from our online catalog
- Check out author bios and background information
- Send e-mail to your favorite authors
- Meet the Kensington staff online
- Join us in weekly chats with authors, readers and other guests
- Get writing guidelines
- AND MUCH MORE!

Visit our website at
http://www.zebrabooks.com